WHAT YOU WISH FOR

A PSYCHOLOGICAL SUSPENSE THRILLER

N. L. HINKENS

This is a work of fiction. Names, characters, organizations, places, events and incidents are either products of the author's imagination or are used fictitiously. For more information about the author, please visit **www.normahinkens.com**

Published by Dunecadia Publishing, California

ISBN: 978-1-947890-49-7

Cover by: https://www.derangeddoctordesign.com/

Editing by: https://www.jeanette-morris.com/first-impressions-writing/

1

SAGE

Sage sipped her black coffee in the cramped back office at Thrifty Tails as her ailing computer whirred to life. A flicker of shame crept up the back of her neck when she remembered the compromising photo that had landed in her inbox a few weeks earlier. Disturbed and perplexed, she found herself staring into her seventeen-year-old, kohl-rimmed, glazed over eyes as she raised a shot glass to the camera. Another night spent drinking and shooting up with her bad boy drug-dealer boyfriend, Jared Brogan. Not that she recalled that specific night—there had been far too many of them, all blurring into one long year of regret.

The message in the body of the email made the sender's intent clear: *the price of silence is $5,000.* Sage had fired off a reply, demanding to know who had sent the email, and threatening to go to the police. She'd regretted it immediately. The message she received in response left her even more shaken.

You already went to the police, snitch! I know some people who would be very interested to hear about that.

Sage hadn't wanted to comply, but she'd paid up, hoping it would be the end of the matter. But it was only a taste of things to come.

The demands continued, and her credit card balance had ballooned in the space of a few weeks. She'd switched to paperless statements to make sure Andrew didn't discover the mess she was in. It felt hopeless, like she was trapped in a maze with no foreseeable way out. What choice did she have but to keep paying her blackmailer until she could figure out who was behind it? She couldn't risk exposing her family to the dangers that came with being ratted out as a snitch to the powerful dealers Jared had been aligned with back then. He had no idea she had sold him out—cooperated with the cops in exchange for full immunity. As a result, Jared was convicted of a drug-related murder and sentenced to forty years. For months afterward, she had kept up the loving-girlfriend facade, visiting him in prison, assuring him she was doing everything in her power to find out who had set him up for a crime he swore he hadn't committed.

Shivering, Sage pulled her fleece tighter around her as she punched in her password and clicked open the POS software to check the latest inventory reports. Back to business—the one she still had some control over.

Rain pounded on the roof of the building, and her thoughts turned to her twenty-year-old daughter, Raven, sleeping rough on the streets of New York in this weather. The irony of it was like a dagger to the heart. She had left that life behind at eighteen, while Raven was only just embracing it. Neither Sage nor her husband, Andrew, could understand their daughter's recent and abrupt decision to drop out of college. Raven had won a full scholarship to Cumbria University and was halfway through her BS in Cybersecurity when she'd suddenly announced she was disillusioned with life and bailing on her degree. She hadn't returned home since, and refused to take their calls, or answer any of their texts.

"Morning Sage," Gloria called out, as she bustled in through the back door and shook the raindrops from her umbrella. "It's dumping out there. I could barely see two feet in front of me."

Sage gave a strained smile. "Freezing cold, too. I'm worried Raven might be out there somewhere in it."

"Oh, honey!" Gloria soothed, shrugging her coat off and hanging it on a hook on the back of the office door. "She's too smart for that."

Sage turned her attention back to her screen. "Drugs make you stupid."

She could say a lot more, but her extensive knowledge on the subject was something she preferred not to broadcast. She envied Gloria her Girl Scout naiveté when it came to worldly vices. With her penchant for all things yesteryear, she was happiest puttering around the thrift store helping customers settle on a vintage purchase, or two, or twelve—she could be very persuasive. Her official title was *manager,* which was a bit of a stretch, being that she was Sage's only full-time staff member. There was no one to manage other than the occasional part-time assistant—a position that came and went as the need arose. Still, replacing Gloria would be a monumental task if she ever decided to retire.

"So, what's on the agenda today?" Gloria asked, slipping a coffee pod into the Keurig.

"We can get started sorting yesterday's drop-offs in the back. We probably won't get much traffic today with all the rain."

"Doesn't the new girl start this afternoon?"

"Yes. Nikki Patterson. Another college student. She says

she went to high school with Raven. Her schedule's a little erratic but we'll take what we can get. I'm not exactly offering an exorbitant hourly rate. I can't believe she's willing to drive all the way from Bridgehaven."

Gloria chuckled. "She must think our furry friends are worth the sacrifice."

Sage arched an eyebrow. "Oddly enough, she's allergic to cats. Climate is more her thing. She's starting a blog decrying the fashion industry for devouring unconscionable amounts of water and energy, and she encourages people to buy preowned clothing so it doesn't go to waste. I didn't have the heart to tell her most of it ends up in the landfill or shipped overseas."

"We do what we can," Gloria said, reaching into the small refrigerator for creamer. "I'll get started out back."

Sage's phone rang, and she bit back a groan of irritation when she saw it was Andrew. They had gotten into it big time last night. It felt like they didn't know how to communicate anymore. When she'd arrived home from work, he was already on edge, nursing a double vodka. He'd accused her of pouring all her love and energy into animal causes, and she had countered that he was too academic to be of any practical use to his family. Admittedly, it was a low blow. She'd been well aware she wasn't marrying a handyman. Andrew was admired by his peers as an insightful thinker and revered by his students as a captivating lecturer. It wasn't the side of him Sage saw. The man she knew was self-absorbed and needy. He hadn't even noticed how rundown she'd been feeling of late. Or maybe he had and didn't care. With a resigned sigh, she slid her finger across the screen.

"I'm worried about Raven," he began, without as much as a greeting or an attempt at an apology.

She pinched her lips together. At least they still had

concern for their daughter's welfare in common. When Raven had dropped out of college, Sage assumed she'd be moving back home. Instead, she informed them she would rather live under a tarp and sent them a picture of her in some dingy bar with some very sketchy-looking characters. A far cry from the type of people Sage had hoped her daughter would surround herself with. Her biggest fear in life was that Raven would follow in her footsteps—footsteps she still kept hidden for good reason.

"I'm worried too," she replied, "But what can we do? Track her down and drag her back home? She's twenty years old, she's free to live wherever she wants—clearly, that's not with us."

"Can you blame her?"

Sage huffed in annoyance. "What's that supposed to mean?"

"You're never home. You're always off speaking at some animal activist event or another, if you're not holed up in that rat trap you call a store."

"Just because you're too much of a germaphobe to set foot inside a secondhand clothing store, doesn't mean Thrifty Tails has no redeeming purpose. Some of us believe in the philosophy of helping. And if you bothered to read our online reviews, you'd know that we get high praise for cleanliness and organization. But you didn't call to talk about my store and, apparently, you didn't call to apologize either. We both know Raven's going to do what Raven wants to do. End of discussion. So why are you really calling?"

A tense silence stretched out. Frustration seeped through Sage. She had work piling up.

"*Andrew?*"

"Because I need you!" he exploded. His voice dropped to a whisper. "One of my students has gone missing."

2

ANDREW

"I'm sorry to hear that," Sage replied, sounding more miffed that he had changed the subject than affected by his news. "How do you know he's missing?"

"She—her name's Jemma Knight." Andrew squeezed his eyes shut, trying not to sound like he was quaking inside. If ever he needed his wife's support, it was now. But in light of his behavior, he was undeserving of it. "Her family hasn't heard from her in several days. They asked the police to do a welfare check. No one in her apartment complex has seen her coming or going in the past forty-eight hours."

"I'm sure she's fine," Sage replied in a clipped tone. "As you and I are painfully aware, young women have a mind of their own. You need to let this go, Andrew. You get so wrapped up in every little drama in your students' lives—if they're not in your office crying because they're homesick, they're whining over grades."

He gripped the phone tighter in his fist, staring at the growing pile of assignments on his desk waiting to be graded. He was having difficulty focusing on anything other than the heart-stopping reality that Jemma was missing. If the facts were different, letting it go would be a reasonable response. But he couldn't afford to raise Sage's suspicions. He needed to take his hysteria down a notch to a level more compatible with a legitimate scholarly relationship. "You're right. It just ... made me think of Raven, that's all."

"The rain made me think of her today, too," Sage replied, her tone softening momentarily. She cleared her throat. "I ... have to go, Andrew. Gloria's waiting on me."

He mumbled a goodbye, but his wife had already ended the call, severing the lifeline he'd hoped she would throw him. It felt as though all she ever did anymore was whisk him away like he was dirt beneath a broom, which was why he was in the predicament he was in.

It had begun innocently enough, with a fleeting glance across a crowded lecture hall. Later that afternoon, Jemma Knight had shown up during office hours with a few innocuous inquiries about class assignments and course content. They ended up spending over an hour talking. Each time she threw back her head and laughed at something Andrew said, he found himself fantasizing about tracing his finger over her glossed lips that so effortlessly curved into a smile at the slightest provocation—a stark contrast to Sage's semi-permanent pout of disapproval of late.

Jemma, in turn, had been taken by his intellect and charisma, or so she'd told him in his arms a few weeks later. He knew he was crossing a demarcation line into a minefield that had the potential to blow up his entire life, but the sting of Sage's neglect, coupled with Raven's abandonment, had led to an insatiable craving to be idolized.

Predictably, the high hadn't lasted. Haunted by the specter of guilt, he had come to his senses last week, and broken things off—using the situation with Raven as his excuse. "I owe it to Sage to patch up our relationship and help save our daughter." Deep down, it was what he wanted most but, as he'd feared, Jemma didn't take it well.

"I need you, too, Andy," she had cried as he walked away, leaving her alone on a bench in Laurelville Park in New Jersey. He hadn't seen her since, and now she was missing. Guilt alternated with waves of anger. He should have broken it off with her more gently. It wasn't his fault. She was overreacting. Her disappearance was a stunt to get his attention, it had to be. The alternative—that she'd harmed herself—didn't bear thinking about. Yet it plagued his thoughts, day and night. Selfishly, he couldn't help worrying that she might have left behind a note outing him as the reason she didn't want to go on living.

Groaning, he dragged his hands through his hair, then reached for his weathered briefcase before heading downstairs to the auditorium to deliver his lecture on The Canterbury Tales. Ordinarily, he was in his element pontificating about medieval English literature and social history, but today his thoughts were disjointed, and he struggled to make it through the material with his usual aplomb. He ended the lecture early and waited until the students were packing up to leave before approaching one of the girls Jemma typically sat with in the front row.

"Sherri," he said, rubbing his chin in a thoughtful manner. "I'm sorry to hear about Jemma. The staff was notified late last night. Are there any updates?"

Sherri shook her head, a woebegone expression on her face. "No. Nothing. The police searched her apartment, but they didn't find anything out of place. She took her purse with her and locked up as usual. We're all freaking out." Sherri blinked at him, doe eyed. "What if someone abducted her?"

Andrew flashed her a sympathetic smile. The odds were close to one in one million. He had looked it up on a computer in the library earlier—not wanting to sully the search history on his personal computer in case the police ever came sniffing around. "I wouldn't worry about it if I were you. I'm sure she'll show up. Maybe she just needed to clear her head before midterms."

Sherri threw him a disparaging look. "Her phone's turned off. Jemma would stay in touch, *if* she could."

Another student approached and stood patiently to one side, presumably with a question about the lecture. Sherri threw her bag over her shoulder and took off before Andrew could stop her.

His heart was still racing by the time he got back to his office after addressing the student's concerns. It had felt like Sherri's eyes were boring right through to the epicenter of his secret—which was ridiculous. Jemma and he had been extraordinarily careful never to meet up anywhere local. They had told no one about their affair. Andrew had warned her repeatedly that he stood to lose everything if it ever came to light. She didn't want that—for either of them.

"We can't have you losing your job, Andy," she had said, tilting her head coquettishly as he held her soft hands in his. "I want to be the wench who marries a professor of medieval English." She loosed a fluttering breath. "Are you *ever* going to leave your wife?"

"She already left me," he had muttered darkly in reply. He and Sage had been good together, until they hadn't. They used to joke about having a preference for the past in common—she with the thrill of the thrifting hunt, and he with his romps through medieval literature. But, in the end, they had each become lost in their own worlds, buried beneath the weight of their secrets.

His phone rang, breaking apart his thoughts like a cattle prod. His eyes widened when Raven's number appeared on the screen. Had she reconsidered her vow never to call them again? Did she want to come home, after all? Maybe sleeping under a tarp in the rain was enough to sour her on the romanticism of a homeless lifestyle and all the challenges that went along with it.

He took her call with an air of trepidation. Raven had been a daddy's girl growing up. They had enjoyed a great relationship right up until the day she had abruptly dropped out of college. Overnight, she had turned on him, rejecting his every overture to talk things over and hash out her issues. He missed her so badly it felt like he was walking around with an open wound.

"Hi, honey. I'm glad to hear from you. Your mom and I were just—"

"Did you do it?" Raven's voice simmered with rage.

Andrew frowned in confusion. Was she talking about him dropping her car insurance? He had made it clear he wasn't going to continue supporting her in her new lifestyle—something he and Sage actually agreed on. "Do what? What are you referring to?"

"Don't play dumb with me!" Raven screamed into the phone. "I know about you and Jemma Knight!"

3

RAVEN

"Where is she?" Raven spat out, barely able to contain her rage.

"I have no idea where—"

"How could you, Dad? She's half your age, only a year older than me! How sick is that? How embarrassed do you think I feel?"

"Raven, I ... " His voice trailed off.

She clenched a fist at her side. Of course, he had nothing to say in his defense—it was indefensible on so many levels. The power imbalance, the unethical behavior, the deception, not to mention the betrayal of his own family.

After a beat of silence, he went on. "Can we meet somewhere and talk about this?"

"You know the answer to that. I've cut ties with you and Mom. I hope I never see either of you again."

"Raven, don't say that. I'm worried about you."

"Maybe you should be worried about the girl who's missing. Did you do something to her?"

"No! Of course not. How can you even think like that?"

"Because I don't know how far you'd go to protect your

cherished reputation. If only your colleagues knew you were as corrupt as the characters in your precious Canterbury Tales!"

"Raven, I made a mistake. A terrible lapse in judgement, I admit. But I've fixed it."

"Yeah, you fixed it, all right—permanently it seems."

"You need to stop talking like that." His voice pitched lower. "I didn't do anything to Jemma."

"Then where is she?"

"I don't know. I broke things off with her a week ago. She didn't take it well. I haven't seen her or talked to her since. She hasn't tried to reach out to me either. I'm worried sick about her." He cleared his throat. "Raven, your mother doesn't know about the affair. It would only hurt her more to tell her now that it's over."

She let out a snort of disgust. "Don't beg me for any favors. There's a lot you two don't know about each other."

She slammed down the phone before he could say another word, too disgusted to continue the conversation. She shouldn't have called him in the first place, but a tiny part of her had been afraid he really might have done something to Jemma Knight. Even if he hadn't, it was his fault she'd run off—no doubt, broken-hearted that he'd ended the relationship. He had been Raven's hero growing up—the kind of charismatic father you could be proud of introducing to all your friends. Hilarious, intelligent, charming—everyone fell under the spell of his sparkling wit. A case of the medieval English emperor's new clothes, as it turned out.

An anonymous note slipped into her backpack had shattered her illusions. *I saw your dad getting cozy with one of his students in a cafe in New Jersey.* Raven had blown it off, at first, but a few days later, a grainy photo had shown up. It looked like him, but the woman his arm was slung around was definitely not her mother. After that, she'd set about surveilling him for several days until she'd confirmed it for herself. She had moved out of the house immediately, and cried herself to sleep that first night, but it would be the last time she would cry over him. He didn't deserve to be called *Dad* anymore. He was Andrew to her from now on—at least to his face.

Sinking back on the luxurious designer leather couch she was seated on, she stared out through the French doors to where the maintenance guy from the pool cleaning service was skimming the already pristine Olympic-sized swimming pool in the backyard. Housesitting for the Baumgartners was a gig she could get used to. Life had been good since she'd stopped speaking to her parents. She was starting a new job next week as a Cybersecurity Solution Analyst, working remote, which was the real reason she had dropped out of college. The starting salary they had offered her boggled the mind, and they would pay for any further education she undertook while working for them. She had given her parents the impression she was living on the street purely for the shock value. The selfie she'd sent them of her doing her best to look sloshed with random strangers in a dive bar had been a particularly satisfying blow. They deserved all the pain she could inflict on them. Their dysfunctional relationship was nauseating. It was time for a new life free from the shadows of their shameful secrets.

She had stumbled onto the shocking skeleton in her mom's closet when she'd hacked into her computer to finish an assignment after the battery on her laptop died. Hard to believe it was her mother in that photograph. She always presented herself as an exemplary citizen, running a thrift store supporting the local animal shelter, volunteering her time to speak to schools and associations to promote animal rights—the epitome of a goody-two-shoes suburban mom. To think that all this time, she'd been hiding a degenerate past. And now, someone from that past was blackmailing her. It had taken some digging—hacking sealed court records, to be specific—but Raven had finally figured out who her boyfriend at the time was. Jared Brogan, a small-time dealer who got forty years for a drug-related murder. And her mom was the snitch who sold him out and walked away in her sanctimonious heels.

Raven squeezed her hands together in her lap as she mulled over the conversation with her dad. She was worried something nefarious had happened to the missing girl. Was it connected to the affair? Dad had sounded genuinely upset. She wanted to believe him when he said he didn't do anything to Jemma. He was a weak man, all show and no substance—she couldn't picture him actually harming anyone.

Her mother, on the other hand, was capable of more than meets the eye.

4

SAGE

Sage donned a pair of gloves and joined Gloria in the back to help sort through the latest stash of donations. It was dirty work, but she enjoyed the process. There was something therapeutic about restoring and repurposing items that had once held sentimental importance and were now deemed garbage. They got their fair share of other people's trash in the mix, but they'd had a few exciting gems show up as well—everything from a live parakeet in a cage to a prosthetic arm.

"Almost time to open up," Sage said, taking off her gloves and stashing them on the shelf behind her. They had worked efficiently for the past hour and managed to process most of the new donations. Her muscles were cramping too much to keep going.

Gloria nodded. "Go ahead. I'll finish up this last box."

Sage turned on the lights in the store and flipped the closed sign to open, then did a quick walk-through to make sure everything was in order. The rain had eased up, so they might see some customers this morning, after all. She cleaned the whiteboard by the register and added the deal of the week—fifty percent off red-sticker sweaters.

"Keep your eye out for scammers moving the sale stickers to our full price sweaters," Gloria said with a chuckle, when she joined Sage a few minutes later. "I don't know why they bother. It would be easier just to steal stuff. It's not as if we have anything barcoded in here." Her eagle eye roved over the space as she talked, and she moved to straighten a pair of shoes on display.

"Maybe it's the thrill of outsmarting us," Sage replied, swallowing the lump in her throat. She couldn't help wondering if Raven had resorted to stealing to survive. How else was she going to make it with no job and a drug habit to feed? Sage could tell from the faces of the new friends in the photo Raven had sent that they were high as kites—she knew a thing or two about the subject. Turning away from Gloria, she pretended to fiddle with a rack of clothing. Raven wasn't the only one who might have to resort to drastic measures to pull through if things kept going the way they were. If the blackmail requests didn't let up, Sage was going to be out of credit in a relatively short amount of time. How was she going to explain her mounting debt to Andrew? She needed to figure out a way to put an end to the ongoing demands for money before it bankrupted them. The stress was taking a toll on her already compromised health. She was still reeling from her doctor's diagnosis.

A bell jangled on the door, and she looked up to see two middle-aged women enter the store.

"Morning, ladies!" Gloria called out, lighting up at the sight of new faces. "It's a wet one today, isn't it?"

While the three women commiserated over the rain, Sage took the opportunity to check her phone. Her heart leapt when a message from Raven popped up. *Did you know one of Andrew's students is missing?*

Andrew's students? What was that about—another pointed way of distancing herself from her parents? Sage thought for a minute, before responding. She didn't want to say anything to aggravate her daughter. She hadn't been in touch for weeks, and it was a strange topic to reconnect over. But, at this point, Sage would take whatever scraps she could get.

Yes, Dad told me. He's very concerned about her.

It took a few minutes before Raven responded.

I bet he is. He's the reason she's missing.

Sage's mouth dropped open. She stared at the text, dumbstruck, before frantically messaging her daughter back.

"Excuse me, ma'am, do you have this in a larger size?"

Sage's head jerked up to see one of the women who had come in a few minutes earlier holding up a floral blouse on a hanger.

She pasted on a practiced smile. "I'm afraid not. Everything we have is donated, so what you see is what you get."

"Hmm, I might be able to squeeze into it," the woman said dubiously, holding it over her ample bosom.

"Just so you know, we have a no returns or exchanges policy, but you're welcome to try it on." Sage gestured to the fitting room.

"Too cold for that today," the woman grumbled. She dropped the blouse on the counter and pulled out her purse. "Oh well, at least I'm supporting the animal shelter. I'll give it to my daughter if it doesn't fit me."

"I'm sure she'll love it," Sage replied, ringing her up. She only hoped her customer's daughter was nowhere near her size, or the blouse was destined to live out the rest of its days on a hanger.

The minute the two women exited the store, Sage fired off several more messages to Raven, but she didn't respond.

Sage's skin prickled as she tried to decipher the hidden meaning in her daughter's text. *He's the reason she's missing.* What was she insinuating? Was this another one of her tactics to hurt them? She kneaded her brow as she thought back to her conversation with Andrew earlier. He *had* seemed unduly worried about the girl—Jemma something or other. But it was hardly the first time a kid had gone AWOL from one of his classes. Maybe he'd given her a bad grade or something. Students dropped out all the time for the stupidest reasons. Was this different in some way? *I need you!* There had been an undertone of desperation in Andrew's voice, and she had totally blown him off. She'd been too consumed with her own problems.

She didn't want her marriage to fail, but was she hiding so many secrets that she was pushing Andrew away? Sage liked to portray herself as the strong one, the consummate activist, large and in charge. Admitting she needed him too, felt like failure. A cold shiver rippled over her shoulders.

What else had her husband been trying to tell her?

5

SAGE

Nikki Patterson showed up early at one-thirty p.m., eager to start her first shift."You don't mind if I blog about my work experience, do you? I'm always trying to educate the public on sustainable living."

She was a serious-looking girl with heavy bangs and glasses, apparently, unafraid to speak her mind—an admirable trait in Sage's eyes.

"Not at all. I'll take all the free advertising I can get. Let me show you around the place and give you a quick overview of how things work. My manager, Gloria Webber, is still at lunch. We weren't expecting you until two. You'll be working mostly with her while you're learning the ropes. She's a veteran of the thrifting world."

"Sounds great," Nikki replied, following her out to the back of the store. "I'm a big proponent of recycling everything. We shouldn't be throwing anything away in this day and age."

Sage raised her brows a fraction. Idealism could become its own straitjacket, but Nikki would learn to make concessions in time. "It's certainly a noble goal. Just so you know, I offer a twenty percent employee discount in case you decide to shop here. Okay, here are our sorting bins where we organize all the donations that come in. You did bring a pair of reusable gloves, right?"

Nikki gave an enthusiastic nod. "Yes, but I'm not afraid to get my hands dirty."

"It's actually more of a safety issue. You might come across items with sharp edges or broken glass, and you don't want to get a spider bite when you're digging through bags of donations that have been sitting out in the carport overnight."

Nikki's eyes widened behind her glasses. "I'm not a fan of spiders—not that I would kill one, of course."

"Not under my watch!" Sage chuckled, leading her back inside the store. "At Thrifty Tails, we advocate for *all* creatures great and small. The first thing you'll do when you arrive in the afternoons is go through the racks of clothing and make sure everything is in the right section and grouped by size. Things have a tendency to get mixed up when it's busy in the store."

"Does Raven ever help out?" Nikki asked, pushing her glasses up her nose.

Sage sucked in a breath, calibrating her reply. She had no intention of maligning her daughter in front of a former classmate. "Raven's busy with her own life."

"She's at Cumbria, too, right?"

Sage gave a high-pitched laugh. *Was*. "Yes. She's ... taking a semester off."

"Really?" Nikki's eyes gleamed with heightened interest. "Is she studying abroad?"

The bell jangled and an elderly man walked in, sparing Sage a convoluted explanation of Raven's disappointing lifestyle choices.

"Is today senior discount day?" the man bellowed.

"That would be Tuesdays." Sage flashed him a smile. "But we do have a half-price sale on sweaters today, and a clearance rack in the back."

The man gave a disgruntled wave of his cane and exited the store just as Gloria walked in.

"Hello. You must be Nikki. I'm Gloria Webber," she said, shaking her hand enthusiastically. "You beat me here."

Nikki smiled primly at her. "My class ended early, so I thought I'd come straight to work."

Gloria stashed her purse behind the counter. "Where are you going to school?"

"Cumbria. I'm an environmental science major."

"That's wonderful. Sage's husband, Professor Golding, teaches at Cumbria."

Sage thought she detected a smirk flickering over Nikki's lips before she adjusted her expression to one of polite admiration. "Yes, I know. A friend of mine was in his class. Everyone raves about him."

Sage fiddled with her sleeve, trying to strike a casual tone. "Do you ... know the missing girl who's been in the news?"

"Not personally, but I had a class with her last semester. Everyone knows who she is. Long, blonde hair, babydoll blue eyes. All the guys were drooling over her. We didn't have much in common. She was one of those fashionista types, didn't care squat about the environment." Nikki frowned. "I hope nothing's happened to her, though. There are so many creeps hiding in plain sight these days."

A cold chill went down Sage's spine. *He's the reason she's missing.* What had Raven been trying to tell her?

A small group of customers came in and began rifling

through the clothing racks. Sage seized on the distraction to excuse herself.

"Gloria, why don't you get Nikki started on doing a full reset of the baby clothing and I'll take care of these customers?"

She couldn't stop shaking as she watched Gloria usher Nikki over to the far end of the store. Meeting someone who knew Jemma, even indirectly, made this so much more real. The possibility that her husband had something to do with a young girl's disappearance was a terrifying prospect. What did Raven know that Sage didn't? Or was her daughter just trying to goad her? Would Andrew really risk his distinguished career over a student? Hundreds of pretty girls had sat in his lectures over the years—why now? Even as she asked herself the question, the answer was staring her right in the face. The more she had accomplished for her cause, the less time she'd had to fawn over him and his career. Andrew needed to be admired. It was rocket fuel to his ego. She didn't have the energy anymore to do both.

Thanks to an unexpected flurry of customers, the remainder of the afternoon flew by. Nikki proved to be a quick learner and an enthusiastic worker—hopefully, she would stick around longer than the last one had. After locking up the store, Sage hurried out to her car, eager to get home and confront Andrew. She didn't know where they would go from here if her worst fears were confirmed, but she couldn't live in this emotional limbo.

Back at the house, she poured herself a sparkling water, then took some chicken and broccoli from the fridge and set about making dinner. While the Chicken Divan casserole baked in the oven, she pulled out her phone to scroll through the animal justice accounts she followed on Instagram, liking and commenting here and there. Her phone pinged with an incoming message. This had better not be Andrew telling her he was going out for drinks with a colleague. She should have texted him to make sure he'd be home for dinner tonight, but she hadn't wanted to give him a chance to prepare a defense. Opening up her messages app, she saw a text from an unknown number.

The cost of betrayal coming back to bite you? $5,000.

6

ANDREW

Andrew turned on the radio to catch the local news as he drove home from work. Just as he'd feared, all the focus was on the missing local girl.

The search continues this evening for missing twenty-one-year-old college senior, Jemma Knight. She left her apartment at approximately seven-thirty p.m. last Thursday night and hasn't been seen since. Her mysterious disappearance—"

He killed the rest of the broadcast. He couldn't listen to it anymore. They were only repeating all the same information anyway. His skin itched beneath his shirt collar. The gravity of the situation was only just beginning to sink in. What if this wasn't a stunt Jemma was pulling to win him back? His mind thrummed with a million questions and fears. What if something really had happened to her? Could he become a suspect?

Somehow, Raven had got wind of his relationship with Jemma. She had screamed down the phone at him like a banshee. When he'd insisted he had no idea where Jemma was, she'd hung up. She had sounded drunk, or maybe she was high on something. He could only hope she was too entangled with her new life and loser friends to take it any further. He dragged a hand through his hair. Being outed by his daughter had felt almost as bad as cheating on his wife. He was no one's hero anymore.

How had Raven found out about them? He and Jemma had been careful to communicate using prepaid phones, but there was always a chance their clandestine affair might become public, even now that he'd ended it. If the police began digging, they might find something to link him to her. The thought made him break out in a sweat. He hadn't signed any of the sappy cards he'd given her, but he hadn't tried to disguise his handwriting either. It might be enough to nail him.

He pulled into the garage and parked his Lexus hybrid next to Sage's Subaru, resting his head on the steering wheel as he tried to calm his racing thoughts before going inside to face his wife. He needed to portray a measured response to the situation. One of his students was missing—naturally, he was going to exhibit some measure of interest in the case, but he couldn't come across as obsessed or devastated, nothing that hinted at guilt. *I need you*, had come out of his mouth before he'd been able to stop it. A heartfelt cry—but dangerously dramatic.

With a heavy sigh, he reached into the backseat for his briefcase. He'd almost rather sleep in his Lexus, but he had to face Sage sooner or later.

"Something smells good in here," he remarked, hitching his lips into a smile as he stepped into the kitchen.

Sage glanced up at him from her phone, her face unusually blanched of color. "I made Chicken Divan."

"Great. I'll just wash my hands and be right there." For a

moment, he considered giving her a peck on her rigid cheek, but he hadn't done that in months. It would feel unnatural, like kissing a corpse. Another bonding ritual abandoned by the wayside as their relationship had taken a nosedive. He took his time in the bathroom, mentally preparing a few funny anecdotes from his day to share over dinner. Inevitably, Sage would ask about the missing girl, but he wasn't going to be the first to bring it up. *Not desperate* and *not obsessed*, he mouthed to himself in the mirror.

Sage was already seated at the table by the time he got back to the kitchen. He pulled out his chair and sat down in front of a steaming plate of casserole. "How was the thrifting business today?" he asked, reaching for his fork.

"Productive. I hired a new assistant. She started this afternoon."

He nodded and smiled as he chewed his food, discomfited by the way Sage's eyes were boring into him.

"She knows Jemma Knight," Sage went on. "She took a class with her. Sounds like she's quite the looker."

He reached for his water to swallow the food that had suddenly become wedged in his throat. "What's your new hire's name?"

"Nikki Patterson, but I'd rather talk about Jemma Knight."

His pulse pounded in his ears. He let out a small sigh, trying to strike a balance between nonchalant and concerned. "It's a sad situation. No new updates, unfortunately. I spoke to one of the girls she sits with in my lectures, and nobody's heard from her. The police searched her apartment, but they didn't find anything concerning. Her friend said she took her purse with her, so that's a good indication she wasn't abducted, at least."

Sage shoved her plate aside and folded her arms on the table in front of her. "How well do you really know her, Andrew?"

He could feel the heat rising up the back of his neck. She knew something. Had Raven told her about the affair? He gritted his teeth. She'd been livid when she'd called him. She must have phoned her mother the minute she'd hung up on him. He would have to pick his way through this minefield carefully—determine how much Sage knew before he spilled his guts. "She's in my medieval literature class. What are you getting at?"

"Are you sleeping with her?"

He flinched at the directness of the question. He was more accustomed to dancing around the issues in their marriage than confronting them head on. But if there was any hope of restoring their relationship, it would have to begin with coming clean about what he'd done.

Abandoning any pretense at enjoying the casserole, he tossed his silverware on the plate. "No. I mean ... not anymore." He let out a shuddering breath. "We had a brief fling. I'm so sorry, Sage. It was utterly stupid of me, and wrong, and I regret it with every fiber of my being. But it's over. I ended it a week ago."

He could almost feel her seething, the table vibrating beneath her elbows, her ragged breathing the only sound in the hush that had fallen between them.

"How could you!" she cried, breaking the agonizing silence. Her tone was scathing, but there was a certain vulnerability in it, too. She looked scared, like a lost child unsure of how to find their way home.

"Sage, I'm going to do everything I can to make it up to you. I'm truly sorry."

She tightened her lips and glanced away. "Raven knows. She sent me a text."

Andrew grimaced. *Of course she did!* But could he blame her? He had broken his daughter's trust, too. "I never meant for it to happen. It was just one of those things. You were so caught up with your activism—gone most nights in the week to some function or another. We were living like roommates. It doesn't make it right, but if you can find it in your heart to forgive me, we can put this behind us and start over."

"Are you serious?" She stared at him as though he'd just told her he was a double agent for an alien race. "The student you were sleeping with is missing. And you want to *put it behind us*? She's someone's daughter."

He raised his hands in a placating gesture. "I didn't mean it like that. Don't make me sound like I'm some kind of heartless monster. Of course, I'm concerned about her but—"

"But nothing! You need to go to the police, Andrew—right away. You ended an affair with the girl, and she disappeared immediately afterward. What if she's harmed herself?"

He rubbed his hands over his face. "I can't go to the police. I'll become the number one suspect in her disappearance. I'm sure she'll show up safe and sound. She probably just took off to clear her head."

"It doesn't matter. You're the reason she's missing. Don't you see that? You have to go to the authorities and tell them the truth. If you don't, I will."

"But I'll lose my job—my whole career will be gutted. How will we pay our mortgage?"

"I'm not thinking about us, right now. I'm thinking about

that young girl you dumped. She could be dead for all we know."

"She's not the only young girl we have to think about. If you go to the police, we'll lose our daughter forever. Whatever chance we have of winning Raven back, it's not going to happen if she thinks I killed someone."

7

SAGE

Sage stared at the ceiling for a long time after Andrew had fallen asleep. She kept going over their conversation in her mind, analyzing it, but finding it fell short of offering her any real hope of reconciliation. He had begged for forgiveness, and insisted he still loved her, but the only time she'd heard any passion in his voice was when he was lamenting the possibility of his precious career being derailed. As usual, Andrew was acting in his own self-interest—*acting* being the operative word. She wasn't going to allow herself to be played for a fool any longer. It was time to face the fact that their marriage had too much dry rot in it to be salvageable. Infidelity was a bridge too far.

Eventually, she gave up trying to fall asleep and went downstairs to make herself a cup of chamomile tea. In the silence of the kitchen, she continued to brood over Andrew's betrayal. *I need you!* She snorted as she reached for her mug. The only reason he needed her was for the optics of having his wife by his side through this crisis. But she couldn't be there for him when he couldn't be there for her. He hadn't once asked how she was holding up, even though it was obvious she wasn't sleeping well, not to mention losing weight—the cumulative effect of the stress of the mounting doctor's appointments she was trying to keep up with.

Raven had told her Andrew was the reason Jemma was missing, but what did that mean? Sage didn't actually believe he had harmed the girl. She would turn him in herself if she thought any different. Jemma was likely sulking at a friend's place, bent on making her professor suffer for breaking up with her instead of filing for divorce. Still, it was immoral in every sense of the word for him to refuse to go to the police and own up to the affair—for the sake of the poor girl's parents, if nothing else. He was too worried about his precious reputation, which only made the whole sordid affair more despicable in her eyes. She had married a coward as well as a cheat.

As she sipped her tea, she fantasized about making elaborate plans to out him—sending invitations to all their friends and family to a surprise champagne reception, then toasting Andrew's infidelity in front of them all. She could almost feel the snap of electricity in the air as shocked friends and family members turned their heads in unison to look at the tongue tied, red-faced professor in their midst.

Grimacing, she got to her feet and carried her mug over to the sink. As enticing as it sounded, she would have to scrap the party idea, she was too broke to host one. Maybe she should mail out *Happy Divorce To Me* cards to all their friends and family with a photo of babydoll, blue-eyed Jemma on the front—start a new trend. She rubbed her hands briskly over her face, erasing the notion. Too inappropriate—at least until the missing girl resurfaced. That left her with the least desirable option of giving Andrew a chance to repair their marriage. Not that she could think of anything he could do to salvage it, at this point. He was right about one thing though. They both wanted to see Raven in a better place. If Andrew was arrested in connection with Jemma's disappearance, Raven might make good on her threat to disown them entirely. But relationships weren't the only thing weighing on Sage's mind tonight.

She fished her phone out of the pocket of her robe and reread the latest message she had received.

The cost of betrayal coming back to bite you? $5,000.

Whoever was behind this, they weren't going to relent. It had to be someone she knew—they had her email and phone number, and they knew what she'd done—suspected, at least. Jared was in prison, so that ruled him out. At first, she hadn't been able to come up with any other prospects, but the more she thought about it, the more she began to suspect her ex-best friend, Marina Garber. Marina had dated Jared for almost a year in high school, until he'd dumped her for Sage. Their friendship had suffered a fatal blow as a result, and it had left a festering wound of betrayal. Marina had accused Sage of giving Jared up to the cops, and threatened to expose her, but she was too scared of the dealers herself to follow through on it. Sage frowned at the text on her phone. Had old grudges resurfaced after all this time? Was that what the blackmail was all about?

"Hey! What are you doing up?"

Her head jerked around at the sound of Andrew's voice. He was leaning in the doorway, arms folded, blonde hair sticking up like straw, eyeing her sleepily—irritatingly attractive without trying.

Sage pressed her lips together in a disapproving line. "I couldn't sleep. Muscle cramps again." *Not that you've noticed.*

Andrew padded barefoot over to the table and pulled out the chair next to her. "I know you're brooding over what I did. You have every right to your pound of flesh, but it will be a lot easier to sleep if you can find it in your heart to forgive me."

"Don't be facetious, Andrew. It's not that simple."

He reached for her hand, but she snatched it away before he could grab it.

She tented her fingers and arched an accusing brow. "Tell me something, how did it feel holding hands with Jemma Knight?"

Andrew leaned back in his chair and groaned. "Don't play therapist with me. I told you it was a dumb mistake. She means nothing to me. I'm here because I want to be here—with you, where I belong. We both know I'm far from perfect, but surely our marriage means enough to you to make it worth fighting for."

Sage shook her head slowly. "I'm not sure it does. Not if you can't go to the police and own up to what you've done. I don't want to live with a liar."

Andrew stared at her for a long moment. "What about our daughter?"

"We'll always fight for her. But let's not fool ourselves that she's going to come home any sooner if we stay together."

Andrew scratched the stubble on his chin. "I'm not tracking. What are you saying, Sage?"

"It's over. We're over. This is the end of the road for us."

8

ANDREW

Andrew sat at his desk with his head in his hands, trying to let it all sink in. His marriage was over, and his fear that something had happened to Jemma was mounting. It had been five days since she'd disappeared and the search had turned up nothing, so far. He had half-expected to hear from her by now: an email begging him to get back together with her, or a desperate phone call late at night—but nothing. His apprehension that something in her apartment would lead the police to him had reached fever pitch. Every time he heard a knock on his office door, he broke out in a sweat. When he wasn't delivering a lecture, he was tormented by visions of interrogation rooms and news headlines asserting his guilt. *Acclaimed professor linked to missing girl's disappearance.* If the truth of his affair with Jemma were ever to come to light, his colleagues would fall on the news like piranhas. The academic world that had once held him in high esteem would be equally passionate about shunning him. From there, it would only go downhill. His career would be shredded in a heartbeat.

Paranoia was taking over his every waking thought like a creeping fungus. In a frenzied attempt to cover his tracks, he had deleted all the messages on his burner phone, then destroyed it with a hammer before disposing of the pieces in a dumpster. He had also burned the photograph Jemma had gifted him of herself for Valentine's Day, as well as the handwritten cards she'd given him. Thankfully, he'd had enough sense to refuse her repeated requests to take a selfie of them together. He had carefully orchestrated their clandestine interactions. Any other memories of their illicit affair were safely locked within the vault of his mind.

Or were they? He frowned, scratching his forehead almost raw. How had Raven found out about him and Jemma? He needed to get a hold of her and figure out how much she knew. Had she seen them together? Heard a rumor? If she had gabbed to Sage about their affair, there was a chance she would talk to other people too. He had to shut her down before she did irreparable damage. He would give her whatever she wanted if she agreed to keep a lid on it. Surely, she understood the danger he would be in if the police suspected him of harming a student. He groaned out loud. Why was he even thinking this way? There was no evidence Jemma was dead—no suicide note, no blood, no weapon, no sign of a struggle, no discarded clothing.

The other thing worrying him was that Sage had threatened to go to the police and tell them about the affair. He had managed to persuade her to hold off, for now. But he wasn't sure she could be trusted to keep her mouth shut if too many more days went by without Jemma showing back up.

There was a tap on the door and Andrew's head jerked up, instant panic gripping him. Office hours were over. It couldn't be a student. Surely it wasn't the police. Had they managed to connect him to Jemma already? He straightened up, hastily smoothing out his hair, reminding himself, for the umpteenth time, not to act desperate or obsessed. "Come in!"

The door opened and Carmen Flores, associate professor of English and Linguistics stepped into the room. She flopped her considerable frame down in the chair opposite him and eyed him accusingly. "I missed seeing you at lunch. Don't give me some Keto diet spiel. You've been hiding out like a hermit crab in your office all day. That's not like you. What's going on?"

Andrew let out a long, relieved breath. When it came to unsolicited visitors, Carmen was infinitely preferable to the cops. "Just been busy, that's all."

She angled her face, the picture of curiosity. "Give me a break, Andrew. I've known you now for eleven—twelve years. You look like you're headed to the executioner's block. Why the long face?"

He raised his hands in a gesture of helplessness. "Fine! The truth is, my marriage is kaput. Or so Sage has informed me."

Carmen furrowed her brow. "You said that like you had no idea it was coming."

"I didn't—not until a couple of nights ago. She wants me to move out."

"I'm sorry to hear that. You can tell me it's none of my business, but is there someone else?"

Andrew flashed her a startled look, his heart pounding in his chest. "What? No! I'm not seeing anyone."

Carmen gave a sheepish laugh. "I meant on her end."

"Sage? No, not a chance. She's far too busy with all her animal activist activities. It's wearing her out, if you ask me.

She's been so preoccupied lately, she barely acknowledges me anymore."

A small smile tugged at one corner of Carmen's lips. "Is that *all* she's busy with? I mean, how would you know what she's up to when she's gone? Seems like she's always off at some speaking engagement or fundraiser."

Andrew averted his eyes. If only Carmen knew who the real cheater was. And who he had cheated with. "I suppose you do have a point."

Carmen smoothed out her skirt and got to her feet. "She should be careful if she's playing the field. You never know who you're going to come across nowadays. Look at that poor Jemma Knight. I'd bet money they're going to find her body any day now."

Andrew gulped and rubbed his sweating palms on his pants. "Why do you say that? She might have dropped out. You know how these kids are—the pressure gets to them, and they bail from one day to the next."

"No way she dropped out. She was a senior, an honors student." Carmen wiggled her dark brows suggestively. "Rumor has it she was secretly seeing someone."

Andrew blinked rapidly. He suddenly felt like he was going to pass out, which would be a very bad thing to do—a physical manifestation of guilt. "Where ... where did you hear that?"

"Didn't you read the staff update? I guess you really have been busy today. The dean received an anonymous email last night. Apparently, Jemma was spotted in New Jersey with an older man."

9

RAVEN

Raven had been on the fence about sending the email to the dean, but someone had to nudge the investigation in the right direction. She was confident the university would be obligated to follow through and pass the tip on to the police. She couldn't in good conscience let her father evade the consequences of his actions with his walking-on-water reputation intact. With that out of the way, she could now turn her attention to the more significant problem of what to do about her mother.

Only a couple of weeks ago, she would have been adamant that Sage Golding, savior of even the lowliest of spiders, was the last person who would harm someone, but armed with the information she had uncovered, she had revised her opinion. If her mom knew about the affair, she might have taken matters into her own hands. Maybe she was the reason Jemma was missing. Her mother's nefarious past, combined with her zeal for any cause she latched onto, made her an intimidating foe to go up against. She had been a fierce advocate for her daughter growing up, but also a demanding coach. Raven smiled to herself. Let's see if her tiger parenting had paid off.

She pulled her laptop toward her, deliberating on her next steps. Hopefully, her cryptic message blaming her dad for Jemma's disappearance had already sent her mother spiraling into panic mode and rocked her picture-perfect world. No doubt, she was petrified Raven would broadcast news of the affair. It was a start, but she wasn't finished yet.

As she logged in, the doorbell chimed throughout the house. She set her laptop aside with an irritated sigh. She had anticipated housesitting the Baumgartners' mansion to be more of a retreat than it was turning out to be. The wealthy had a revolving door of strangers taking care of every facet of their lives. If it wasn't the pool service showing up, it was the housekeeping staff, or the gardeners lurking outside every window, the dry cleaning service dropping off curtains, the security team checking the premises, the personal assistant picking up files from the home office, or even the chef stocking her up on groceries—she had politely declined his services to cook her meals. On and on it went. She couldn't begin to imagine what it was like when the family was home, and the masseuse, the hairdresser, and the personal fitness trainer got added to the list. On the totem pole of servants, the house sitter's job was a lowly one —she was mostly tasked with answering the door.

Pasting on a smile, she made the long trek to the oversized pivot front door and waited until the biometric scanner automatically opened it on her behalf.

"Hello Raven," the young woman standing on the front steps said.

She blinked, taking a minute to study her face. There was something familiar about her, but her heavy fringe and shades were hiding half her features.

The woman smirked as she removed her sunglasses. "It's Nikki Patterson, from high school. Aren't you going to invite me in?"

Raven's spine stiffened. This was not someone she had expected to run into again, and for good reason.

"What are you doing here?" she hissed.

Nikki craned her neck to get a better view of the sprawling mansion. "Currently, admiring your new digs. I was hoping to get a tour."

"How did you get through the gate?"

"The pool service just left. I gave them a friendly wave on their way out. They probably thought I was with you."

She took a step forward, and Raven shot out a hand to stop her. But it was impossible to block the expansive doorway.

Nikki easily slipped by into the marble hallway and let out a low whistle. "This place is something else."

"I'm not allowed visitors," Raven snapped.

Nikki shrugged. "Turn off the cameras." She raised a condescending brow. "Given your vast experience in running interference, I'm sure you've already figured out how to tinker with it."

Raven sighed and walked over to a master panel on the wall to temporarily disable the cameras. If the Baumgartners got an alert, she would reassure them it had been a temporary glitch.

She led Nikki into the expansive kitchen and gestured to a leather stool at the soapstone bar, before leaning back against the counter. She folded her arms across her chest, her gaze boring into her unwanted guest. "How did you find me?"

"I bumped into your ex, Tyler. He told me you'd landed a housesitting gig for some wealthy people—

parents of a friend of yours who were overseas. It wasn't hard to figure out which of your friends' fathers was a financier for a Swiss banking corporation." She glanced around her. "Do they have a wine cellar? I could use a drink."

Raven walked over to the built-in refrigerator and retrieved two bottles of water, inwardly fuming that Tyler had gabbed to Nikki. The guy was a loser—she should have sent him packing sooner. She'd only dated him to spite her parents, knowing they would have hated his tattooed, bad boy image. It was a shame she hadn't had the chance to introduce him before she'd kicked him to the curb. She slammed a bottle of water down in front of Nikki. "Why are you here?"

"For old time's sake, although I can't say the memories are happy ones." Her eyes glinted with a flash of anger. "You stole that scholarship from me."

Raven snorted. "Seriously? You're still bitter I won?"

"It should have been mine. I earned it."

"You didn't earn squat! You deleted my original application. Too bad you weren't a better hacker back in the day. I caught it in time to resubmit it. Get over it, Nikki. It's unbecoming to be whining about high school drama at your age."

"What's unbecoming is how much debt I'll be graduating with, thanks to you. A little over a quarter of a million dollars. Enough to buy myself a house in many states."

Raven shrugged. "My advice—transfer. There are a lot more economical places than Cumbria to get a degree."

Nikki drummed her fingers on the counter. "You know what the really sickening part about it is? You're not even there anymore. You dropped out and threw it all away like it meant nothing to you."

"It got me a job."

A sly grin spread over Nikki's face. "Yes, it did. A very well-paid job, I believe. That's what I'm here to talk about."

Raven froze, her water bottle halfway to her lips. "How do you know about my job?"

"I've made it my business to find out everything about you. It's time we settled our differences."

"Fine. Settled. Have a nice life! Now, get out before the homeowners call the security firm."

"It's going to take a little more than a begrudging truce to heal my wounds." Nikki took a sip of water, her gaze flitting around the space. "It would be a nice gesture if you paid off my tuition in return for me keeping my mouth shut about how you hacked into my computer and framed me for cheating on the scholarship essay." A spiteful grin twisted her lips. "Cybersecurity firms take these kinds of things very seriously. You'd be out of your new job in a heartbeat. In fact, I doubt you'd be hired by anyone in the industry ever again."

10

SAGE

Sage left Gloria to manage the front of the store while she took a quick lunch break in the back. As she munched on her sandwich she checked her messages, relieved to find no new demands for money. She still hadn't told Andrew what was going on—if they were headed for divorce, he would find out soon enough.

It had been a few days since she'd asked him to move out and he was no closer to finding somewhere else to live. Considering how popular he was among his colleagues, surely someone could offer him a room or an apartment as a temporary fix. She had a feeling he was dragging his heels, hoping she would relent. However, he had miscalculated the depth of her resolve.

"Hi Sage," Nikki said, coming in through the back door and hanging up her coat. "How's everything going?"

"Good. We were slammed this morning—it's always like that at the start of the month. I haven't had a chance to sort yesterday's drop-offs yet, if you want to get started on those."

"Sure thing."

"Thanks. I'm going to relieve Gloria so she can take her break now."

She zipped up her lunch bag and stashed it next to her purse before making her way inside the store where Gloria was ringing up a customer.

"Have a wonderful rest of your day," she chirped, handing the woman her receipt.

Sage watched her trundle off with her purchases under her arm. "Another happy Thrifty Tails customer. You make it look easy."

Gloria let out a snort. "She was one grumpy granny! She wanted a discount for an imaginary stain on a blouse, said our books were overpriced, and complained about the immodest naked dolls in the plastic bin over by the toys."

Sage laughed. "That's a first."

They swung around in unison at the sound of someone bursting into the store from the back. Nikki skidded to a halt, staring at them, her face drained of color.

Gloria exhaled loudly, fanning herself with her hand. "You about gave me a heart attack, girl! I thought we were being robbed or something."

"Sorry. I ..." Nikki's voice trailed off.

Sage raised her brows a fraction. "What's wrong? Spiders terrorizing the donations bin again?"

"I ... I think you should take a look at this," Nikki stammered.

Gloria threw Sage a knowing look, then lowered her voice. "Go ahead before she has a meltdown. I'll hold down the fort."

Sage flashed her a smile of thanks. "I hope it's not an escaped pet snake or something. I'm pretty sure a reptile would put her over the edge."

She threw a keen eye over the rails of clothing as she

made her way out to the back. She needed to get Nikki out front to start tidying up. Things were looking decidedly messy after their morning rush.

"All right. What's got you so freaked out?" she asked, walking over to the donations staging area.

Nikki pointed to a blue mosaic pot sitting on a beat-up end table. "I found that in a box of miscellaneous decor. There's something inside it. I think it's ... I think it's ashes."

Sage lifted off the lid. She peered suspiciously at the grainy-looking, gray-brown material inside. She wasn't exactly sure what ashes looked like. It could be a pile of sand for all she knew. She sniffed tentatively at it. No odor. Not that it meant anything.

"Do you think it's ashes?" Nikki asked, rubbing her arms forcefully as though chilled to the bone.

Sage smiled reassuringly. "If it is, it's probably someone's pet. A family member cleaning out a deceased relative's place might have inadvertently added it to the pile. Believe it or not, it's not the first time it's happened. Don't worry, I'll take care of it."

She reached for the pot to take it with her to the office, her heart doing double time, despite the reassurance she'd given Nikki. She wasn't exactly sure why, but she felt an urgent need to make the pot disappear. It was incredibly bad timing for it to show up with Jemma still missing. It was making her think paranoid thoughts.

"But what if it's not someone's pet?" Nikki cried. "I mean, what if it's a ... a person?"

A cold thread of fear slithered through Sage. "If it makes you feel any better, I can post a picture on our Facebook page and ask if anyone recognizes the pot."

Nikki blew her fringe out of her eyes, considering the suggestion. "I'd feel better if we turned it in to the police.

They'll be able to test the ashes to find out if they're human or not."

Sage inhaled a calming breath. She couldn't afford to act in an overly defensive manner. The last thing she wanted to do was raise Nikki's suspicions. "One step at a time. Let's wait and see if anyone claims it first."

Nikki reached out a shaky hand to a nearby table to steady herself. "I ... don't feel too good. I need to go home."

Sage bit back a sarcastic response. Nikki had only just arrived to start her shift and she was already bailing on them. Hopefully, she hadn't made a mistake hiring the girl. Discovering the urn—if that's what it was—had rattled Sage too, but reason prevailed. In all likelihood, someone's beloved Fido or Kitty was resting peacefully inside the pot. But maybe it would be better if Nikki went home so she could figure out how to dispose of it. "Okay. Grab your coat. I'll finish up out here."

Nikki wasted no time scuttling out to the parking lot and driving off. Sage deposited the urn in the office and made her way back inside the store to relieve Gloria.

"Well, our part-time assistant discovered an urn full of ashes in the donations, got spooked, and took off for the day." Sage gave a rueful shake of her head. "I told her it was probably just somebody's pet, but nothing I said could induce her to stay."

Gloria rolled her eyes. "This generation is made of cotton wool. Just wait until she stumbles on some yellowing dentures."

Sage chuckled, leaning against the counter by the register. "Go ahead and take your lunch. I'll watch the shop for a bit."

Gloria retreated to the back office, and Sage sank down on the stool behind the register. She had blown off the discovery of the urn, but, in truth, it niggled at her. She didn't know why she was having such morbid thoughts, but death had been on her mind a lot lately. She pulled out her phone to distract herself. Marina still hadn't responded to her text. She might have gotten a new number since high school. It was equally possible she was choosing to ignore her. If she was behind the blackmail demands, she was hardly going to confess to it. Sage had reluctantly wired another five thousand dollars yesterday, not wanting to risk the blackmailer making good on their latest threat to out her.

When Gloria returned, Sage headed out back to start on the donations she'd asked Nikki to tackle. Her muscles felt stiff but she pushed through the discomfort. It was worse at night when the twitching started, making it almost impossible to sleep. She worked methodically through several bags of clothing before pulling out a pale blue puffer jacket. It appeared to be of decent quality. She inspected the label and checked the seams for rips. Her lip curled when she noticed a rusty stain on the left sleeve that looked suspiciously like blood. Why on earth did people send in unwashed clothing? It wasn't as if they ran a laundromat service.

Tossing the jacket to one side, she reached for the next item in the bag and pulled out a pair of ripped designer jeans. Expensive, but also stained. She peered gingerly into the bag to see what else was in there, recoiling in horror at the sight of a heavily bloodstained white T-shirt bunched up like a rag at the bottom of the bag. Her skin began to prickle. She drew her brows slowly together, thinking back to the description of the missing girl on the evening news.

Jemma Knight was last seen wearing a blue puffer jacket and ripped jeans.

11

SAGE

Sage clapped a hand to her mouth to trap the scream threatening to erupt. It couldn't be a coincidence, could it? These were Jemma's clothes—they had to be. But how had they ended up here? And what had happened to her? Judging by the amount of blood on the T-shirt, she had bled out. Had she been stabbed? Shot? She couldn't bear to think about it. The more important question was: who had killed her? Was it possible Andrew could have done something so despicable? Maybe it was an accident. If Jemma had come at him first and he'd tried to deflect the attack, he might have inadvertently killed her in the process.

More frantic thoughts churned like whitewater rapids in her mind. Why had Jemma's clothes been hidden among the donations? She scratched maniacally at her arms, twitching all over as her mood plunged to a new incomprehensible low. What if Andrew was trying to frame her for a murder he had committed? Was this his perverted way of getting revenge on her for calling it quits on their marriage? Her life, already on a downward trajectory, was in complete shambles now. Even the blackmail and her devastating diagnosis paled in significance to this new nightmare staring her in the face.

Her thoughts shifted to the mosaic pot sitting on the desk in her office. A cold fury rose from her belly. Andrew wasn't going to get away with this. He couldn't pin this on her—whatever this was. She would fight back—make sure he was held accountable for what he had done. Thanks to her gloves, she hadn't contaminated the evidence. Hurriedly, she stuffed the soiled clothing back into the bag, then dialed Andrew's number. "I need you to meet me at Thrifty Tails."

"I can't—"

"Now!"

"Why? What's going on?" Andrew's tone was one of tempered irritation. "I have office hours this afternoon."

"Cancel them."

He blew out a long-suffering sigh. "Can you at least tell me what this is about? You've barely spoken two words to me in days and now, all of a sudden, you're demanding that I drop everything and run to your side."

"If you're not here in thirty minutes, I'm calling the police."

"Wait! I just—"

Sage ended the call and slipped the phone into her jacket pocket. Tenting her hands over her eyes, she gritted her teeth. Why was this happening now, on top of all the other problems weighing her down? The only thing worse would be hearing that Raven had died of an overdose in a gutter somewhere. The thought terrified her, but the reality was always there, gnawing at her like a beady-eyed rat. She had to hang in there—someone had to fight for their daughter.

Taking a few deep breaths, she smoothed her hands over

her hair. She couldn't go back inside the store looking like an electrocuted zombie. She needed to pull herself together and not raise Gloria's suspicions that she'd uncovered something far worse than Fido's remains. If Gloria got even an inkling that Sage had discovered bloody clothing too, there was no way she could avoid turning the store into a crime scene.

In the tiny bathroom, she washed her hands obsessively, then practiced smiling in the mirror to relax her features. She prided herself on being self-possessed and in control at her speaking engagements, but nothing could have prepared her for discovering her husband's lover's bloody clothing—possibly her ashes, too. Sage's stomach heaved at the thought. Was this really happening? She dried her hands, then made her way into the store, her expression schooled to one of normalcy.

"Gloria, Andrew is going to stop by. I ... uh, need him to help me move some furniture. Are you okay holding down the fort up front?"

"Of course." Gloria beamed at her. "That's nice of him to help out. Sounds like you two are working things out."

Sage twisted her lips. *If only you knew.* "I wouldn't go that far."

"If you want to work the register until he gets here, I'm happy to keep sorting donations. You look exhausted."

"*No*! I mean, thank you, but I'm almost done. I'd rather just finish up. It will give me a chance to catch up on my podcasts." She gave an overly shrill laugh. She didn't listen to podcasts, but it was the first thing that had come to mind.

Gloria eyed her skeptically as she reached for a T-shirt. "O-kay."

Sage scurried away out of range before her shrewd

manager could pose a more penetrating question. On her way back out, she retrieved the mosaic pot from the office with shaking hands. Ordinarily, she was good at masking her feelings, but there was too much at stake not to be affected by what she'd uncovered. She had to get Andrew to confess to what he'd done. After that, it was a matter of persuading him to go to the police before they came knocking on their door. If he refused, she would turn him in herself. She wasn't going to risk being charged as an accomplice to murder in a story she was certain was destined to make national headlines.

When she spotted Andrew's Lexus pulling up in the back parking area, Sage locked the door to the office to make sure Gloria didn't walk out and surprise them.

Andrew strode over to her, irritation oozing from every pore. "This had better be important. My students have midterms coming up. It's an inopportune time to cancel office hours at the last minute."

Sage fixed him with an icy stare. "This is about one of your students—the missing one, actually."

A deep cleft formed on his brow. "What about her?"

She reached for the plastic bag of clothing on the ground and tipped it out. "I don't know what you did, but you're not pinning this on me."

His lips moved as though to form a sentence that somehow evaporated into thin air. He looked visibly shaken as he squinted at the clothing. "Is that ... blood?"

"Yes. And those are Jemma's clothes."

He threw her a harried glance. "What?"

"You heard me!"

He looked back down at the pile of clothing, trailing a shaky finger over his brow.

"That's what she was wearing when she was last seen,"

Sage said, flinching at the tremor in her voice that betrayed her fear.

"Are you sure?"

She narrowed her eyes at him. "You're a terrible actor."

"Sage, I didn't do anything to her." Andrew's voice rose a panicked notch. "You have to believe me. I don't know anything about this. I would never harm her."

She shook her head slowly. "Somebody did." She reached over and lifted the lid from the pot. "This got dropped off here last night along with the bloody clothing. Does that look like ashes to you?"

Andrew threw her a horrified look, a frenzied sheen forming in his eyes. He let out a moan, swaying back on his heels. "Oh no! No! No! No! What have you done, Sage?" He placed both hands on top of his head, muttering to himself. "I warned her not to come here. She wanted to see what you looked like in person."

Sage grabbed him and shook him until he quit mumbling and focused his gaze on her. "Get a grip, Andrew! I didn't kill your girlfriend, but it looks like someone's trying to frame me. Is it you?"

"No! Are you insane?" Andrew pressed the palms of his hands to his face. "Those can't be ashes. It's probably just sand or gravel. This is Jemma playing a sick joke on me."

Sage stared at him coldly. "You don't get that much blood from a paper cut. The clothing speaks for itself. Someone killed her."

12

ANDREW

Andrew stared at the urn. He felt as though he was suspended in time as he tried to wrap his head around what Sage was telling him. It was too fantastical to think that someone had killed Jemma and was trying to frame his wife for her murder. There had to be another explanation. Could Jemma be behind this? Was it a stunt to punish him, or to coerce him into resuming their relationship? But why would she put her family through so much trauma? Her distraught parents had put out a plea on the evening news for their daughter's safe return. The Jemma he knew wasn't capable of such cruelty. But maybe he didn't know her as well as he thought he did.

"We have to get rid of the clothing," he blurted out. "If someone's trying to set us up, they might have called a tip in to the police already. What other motivation could there be other than to have one of us—or both of us—arrested? It's not as if they're blackmailing us or anything."

Sage's hand flew to her throat. She fiddled with the neck of her blouse, her brow creased with concern. She looked like she was about to say something but then didn't. It wasn't like her to be at a loss for what to do or say. But these were no ordinary circumstances. He had brought this nightmare to her doorstep. It was up to him to fix it. "We need to ... to make a decision," he stammered. Do you want me to handle the clothing? We can't stand out here for much longer without Gloria getting curious about what we're up to."

"We can't just ditch the evidence," Sage said. "Think of her parents. We have to go to the police. You have to confess to the affair."

He locked eyes with her, silently pleading for her to see sense. "If that's Jemma's blood on the clothing, they'll home in on me as their number one suspect. They won't bother looking for the real killer."

Sage frowned. "I suppose I could take the clothing to the police and tell them I found it dumped in with the donations, without mentioning anything else."

Andrew rubbed a hand over the back of his neck. "Too risky. If Raven gets wind of the fact that Jemma's clothing turned up here, she'll out me. Then I'm screwed. I'm pretty sure she already sent an anonymous email to the dean."

Sage threw up her hands. "So, what do we do?"

He paced back-and-forth. "Who else knows about this?"

"Nikki, our new part-timer—she discovered the urn. I tried to pass it off as someone's forgotten pet, but she was pretty distraught about it. She ended up going home early. I told Gloria about it, of course. She took it in her stride. It's not the first donated urn she's encountered."

He frowned. "Do they know about the bloody clothing too?"

Sage shook her head. "No. I found that after Nikki left." She threw a nervous glance over her shoulder, then hurriedly stuffed the clothing back into the bag.

Andrew rubbed his jaw, his gaze drifting to his car.

"Okay, here's what we're going to do. I'll take the bag and drop it off in the donations bin at another thrift store. That way, we're preserving the evidence without throwing me to the wolves for a crime I didn't commit."

Sage wet her lips nervously. At length, she gave a hesitant nod. "What about the urn?"

"You need to take the contents to a lab and have them analyzed. I'm pretty sure it'll turn out to be sand or something like it. If someone killed Jemma, they're hardly going to have her cremated, are they?"

"And if you're wrong?"

Andrew threw her a loaded look. "We'll cross that bridge when we get to it." He bent over to lift the bag of bloody clothing, then hesitated. "Do you have any gloves?"

Sage gestured to the shelf behind him. He lifted down the largest pair, struggling to pull them on, before grabbing the bag. "You might want to get that sample to the lab, sooner rather than later. For everyone's peace of mind."

He jogged over to his car, tossed the bag in the back, then sat for a minute or two googling thrift stores. He didn't want one too close to Thrifty Tails, or one with cameras recording his every move either. After weighing his options, he settled on Second Street Resale in East New York. It was comparable in size to Thrifty Tails, and likely staffed by only a couple of people. He could make his drop discreetly and disappear without engaging anyone.

After parking a block away, he sat for several minutes, reassuring himself that this was the right thing to do. His hunch was that Jemma was conspiring against him, and taking her fury out on his wife, but he couldn't rule out the possibility that something bad had happened to her. Preserving the evidence, while diverting attention away from himself, was the best he could do for her.

Donning his shades and a baseball cap, he slipped his briefcase beneath the seat, grabbed the black trash bag of bloody clothing, and climbed out of his Lexus. He was taking a chance on his car still being intact when he got back to it. This wasn't the best area of town to hang out in. Keeping his head down, he walked at a moderate pace in the direction of Second Street Resale. No one paid him the slightest bit of attention as he casually deposited the bag next to the pile of donations in the alley behind the store. His heart pounded as he retraced his steps.

He had done the right thing. He knew he had. So why did he feel as if he had just sold his soul on the dark web?

As his car came into view, his heart sank.

13

RAVEN

After Nikki left, Raven logged onto her computer and did some unauthorized investigating into her unsolicited visitor. It turned out she wasn't enrolled at Cumbria at all. She was taking classes at some local community college. Go figure! Had she even been accepted to Cumbria? No matter. It didn't change the fact that Raven had indeed falsified Nikki's essay and framed her for cheating. Nikki had insisted she had proof and, until Raven knew otherwise, she would have to tread carefully.

In retrospect, she didn't even know why she'd hacked into Nikki's computer and added a plagiarized paragraph to her essay, other than to prove that she could. High school had been a boring wasteland she'd itched to leave behind. Insufferable people like Nikki Patterson had made it worse. A know-it-all who sucked up to every teacher and talked down to every student. Deleting Raven's scholarship application had been a step too far. Nikki had needed a heavy dose of humiliation, and Raven had delivered a master stroke. It amused her, more than delighted her, that she'd ended up winning the scholarship Nikki had coveted.

Abandoning her laptop, she began pacing up and down the long marble corridors in the Baumgartners' mansion. Her footsteps echoed maddeningly in the cavernous space as she tried to think her way out of this mess. She had finally gotten rid of her nemesis after promising to deposit her first paycheck into Nikki's bank account by the end of the week. Not that she had any intention of following through on it. But it would buy her a couple of days to figure out how she was going to handle this situation. The irony wasn't lost on her that she and her mother were both being blackmailed for past sins. Not the kind of thing mothers and daughters usually bond over, but secrets had made their relationship dysfunctional.

Hunger pangs stabbed at her, reminding her that she hadn't eaten breakfast. She headed to the kitchen and pulled out a carton of eggs from the industrial-sized refrigerator. The Baumgartners' chef had stocked it with an impressive array of expensive cuts of meat and organic vegetables, but an omelet was the height of her culinary wizardry. She was cracking eggs into a bowl when a message came through on her phone.

Jemma's ashes are at Thrifty Tails.

She froze, the eggshell crushing between her fingers and falling into the bowl. *Ashes*! Was Jemma dead? The dense silence in the empty house pressed in around her. Another anonymous message. She had assumed the note she'd found in her backpack about her dad had come from someone at Cumbria, possibly even a colleague hoping to avert a scandal. But this person knew the name of her mother's business, and they had her phone number.

She swallowed the knot of fear lodged in her throat. Was Jemma really dead? And how did this stranger know where her ashes were? Her mind spun in a kaleidoscope of emotions as she thought back to what she'd discovered about her mother's past. Could she have hired someone to dispose of Jemma? Did she still have contacts in the drug world? She shook her head free of the disturbing thought. It was ridiculous to think either of her parents were capable of killing someone, wasn't it? An electric shiver went down her spine. At least, not intentionally.

But it could have been an accident. Maybe her mom had known about the affair before Raven texted her. What if she'd confronted Jemma about it? If things had turned physical, Jemma could have fallen and hit her head. Her mom might have panicked, knowing her past would not bode well for her. Raven pressed her hands to her face. All speculation on her part. She needed proof. First, she had to figure out who the anonymous sender was, and how they knew so much about her parents' secrets.

Gingerly, she began picking the eggshells out of the bowl and tossing them in the trash, before giving up on breakfast and dumping the raw eggs down the garbage disposal. She couldn't face the thought of eating an omelet now. Her stomach was churning enzymatic whirlpools. She gripped the edge of the counter and leaned over it, scrunching her eyes shut. She had no choice but to break her own rules and pay her mother a visit. She needed to look her in the eyes and ask her face-to-face if she'd done something to Jemma Knight. It was the only way to know for sure if she was guilty.

Her decision made, she dressed quickly in her slouchiest clothes and threw her brown leather crossbody bag over her head before making her way out to her car. She didn't exactly look homeless, but she didn't look like she'd slept in a multimillion-dollar mansion last night either. Hopefully, her mother didn't pick up on the discrepancy between her appearance and her purported homeless lifestyle. Her outfit was a little too clean to be convincing, but it would have to do. Time was of the essence. She gritted her teeth as she put the car into gear and backed out of the polished concrete garage. This was all her father's fault. Why, after all these years, had he succumbed to seducing a student—quite possibly the stupidest thing a man in his position could do? The pedestal she'd placed him on for most of her life had crumbled to powder in a single moment of reckoning.

After pulling up outside Thrifty Tails, she parked at the curb, taking a few minutes to compose herself before climbing out. The bell jangled as she pushed open the front door. Gloria glanced up from the rack of skirts she was organizing. Her sparse brows shot up and a broad grin spread across her homely face. "Raven! It's so nice to see you, honey."

She gave a sheepish smile in return. It had been a while since she had last set foot inside the store. No doubt, her mother had told Gloria all about her less-than-desirable lifestyle, but the woman was as welcoming and non-judgmental as ever. "Is my mom here?"

"She is indeed. She's out back sorting donations." Gloria hesitated, a small frown puckering her forehead. "She could use some help. She's worn out, poor thing. The new hire took off early."

Raven nodded and made her way to the back of the store, wrinkling her nose at the distasteful odor of used and discarded goods. She wasn't surprised to hear they had hired another new assistant. None of them lasted more than a few months. Why anyone would want to work in a thrift store was beyond her. On the list of least desirable retail positions, it had to be pretty high up there. She wasn't a germaphobe, like her father, but she did have standards—

which made it all the more surprising that her parents had bought the preposterous lie that she was living on the streets.

"Hello Mother," she said, opening the back door that led out to the donations staging area.

Sage spun around, almost tripping over the bags on the ground next to her. "Raven!" The surprise on her face was mixed with an edge of apprehension. She looked paler and thinner than when Raven had last seen her.

"What are you doing here? I mean, I'm happy to see you, honey. It's just—" Her voice trailed off when she noticed the stony look on Raven's face. "Is everything all right?"

"You tell me," she replied. Her gaze traveled over the donations, landing on a blue mosaic pot sitting on an end table by the wall. Her pulse ratcheted up a notch. She strode over to it and lifted the lid off it before Sage could stop her. Her heart rumbled in her chest as she eyed the contents. Slowly, she turned to face her mother. "Is it her?

Sage threw a nervous glance over her shoulder. "Sssh. Are you crazy?"

Raven slammed the lid back down on the pot. "You didn't even have to ask me who I was referring to, did you? You knew exactly who I was talking about. Because you killed her!"

14

SAGE

"I have no idea what you're talking about." Sage darted a frantic glance at the back door, terrified that Gloria would emerge at any minute and overhear their conversation.

"I'm talking about Jemma Knight, the missing girl *Andrew* had an affair with."

Her stomach knotted. It was hard to hear the sordid truth coming out of her daughter's mouth, and equally difficult to hear her dissociate herself from her father. Was she next in line to be stripped of her hard-earned title of *Mom*? "Don't be ridiculous. I don't know why you would even think I could do something like that."

Raven took another step toward her. Sage flinched. Something in her daughter's expression scared her.

"I think you're capable of a lot more than you pretend to be," Raven answered, her eyes glinting dangerously. "I know a thing or two about your questionable past that you've so carefully tapestried over with your nauseating array of good-deed causes."

A cold sweat broke out over the back of Sage's neck.

She'd been so careful to keep every trace of her regrettable past hidden—she'd never even shared it with Andrew. Raven couldn't possibly know, could she? How had she found out? Those records were sealed. Sage was a juvenile at the time. Then again, her daughter was something of a prodigy when it came to rooting out things best left buried.

"Raven," she said, lowering her voice, "This is neither the time nor the place to have this conversation. Can we go back to the house and talk about it?"

"I'm not going anywhere with you. We're going to have this conversation right here, right now. Otherwise, I'm calling the police and telling them everything." With her jaw set tight, she held her phone aloft as if to drive home her point.

Sage clenched a fist at her side. She could hardly fault her daughter for her intimidation tactics. Hadn't she just done the same thing to Andrew—given him an ultimatum? "All right. Fine. What do you want to talk about?"

"Let's start at the beginning. Why didn't you tell me about your loser drug-dealing boyfriend who went to prison for murder? It's a pretty significant part of your past to leave out, don't you think?"

Sage bristled at her derisive tone. "It has no relevance to me anymore. I left that life behind when I was seventeen and I've never looked back."

Raven folded her arms in front of her. "Apparently, you haven't left it behind. Someone from that past is hitting you up for money in return for keeping their mouth shut about you snitching to the cops. You're the reason your scumbag boyfriend got convicted. You ratted him out to the police."

She gasped. "You hacked into my computer, didn't you? I could have you prosecuted for that."

Raven snorted. "What does it matter? The point is, your

past has caught up with you and you're in trouble. The last thing you need right now is another problem, like Jemma Knight. Did you hire someone to get rid of her—do your dirty work for you? I'm sure you still have a few shady contacts from the delinquent days of your youth."

"You need to stop with this nonsense! I didn't even know Jemma Knight existed until she went missing." She frowned, scrutinizing her daughter. A terrible thought crept slowly up her spine. "How did you know about the ashes anyway?"

"That's irrelevant to our discussion."

Sage grabbed Raven by the arms and shook her. "You're the one who told me about your father's affair. Is this your doing? Are you messing with us, pulling some stupid stunt? Or did you actually do something to that girl?"

"Get your hands off me!" Raven raged, wriggling until she broke free from Sage's grasp. "I don't know what happened to Jemma. That's why I'm here."

Sage raised her palms in a placating gesture and took a step back. "Okay, okay, I'm sorry. Let's both calm down and try talking this through in a level-headed manner. Someone is out to get me. I think they're trying to frame me for murder." She gestured at the pot. "I'm going to take a sample to the lab and have it tested. Your dad doesn't believe it's ashes. He thinks *Jemma* is toying with us."

Raven let out a scoffing laugh. "Of course, he would say that. How many times are you going to allow yourself to be played for a fool by that man? Think about it. He had an affair with a student. If she threatened to talk, he might have lashed out. Maybe he didn't mean to kill her. She could have fallen and hit her head, and he panicked. Everything's at stake—his job, his career, his whole identity. Without it, he's nothing."

Sage inhaled slowly in and out as she considered Raven's

words. She couldn't argue with her reasoning. Was Andrew trying to pull the wool over her eyes? She had let him drive off with that bag of bloody clothing, but where was he really taking it?

"Aren't you going to say something?" Raven huffed. "Or are you just going to keep on defending him?"

"I'm not defending him. Your father had an affair, and it comes at a price. I've asked him to move out. But, without any proof that he's harmed Jemma, I'm not going to turn him into the police."

"That's called obstruction of justice, *Mother*. Why don't you do something I can be proud of, for once?"

Sage glared at her. "I've spent my whole life doing things you can be proud of. Maybe you don't appreciate that, but I've always fought for what I believe in."

"Yes, you have, and you taught me well, which is why I'm going to do what you should have done and turn that murdering philanderer in."

Before Sage could stop her, Raven swooped up the urn from the table and darted off with it.

15

ANDREW

Heat flushed through Andrew's veins as he approached his car. He had taken a huge risk parking here, stupidly hoping for the best. The rear passenger side window was smashed, glass scattered all over the seat. Opening the back door, he confirmed his suspicion. He had stuffed his leather briefcase under the seat so it wouldn't attract attention, but someone's eagle eye had spotted it peeking out. He twisted his lips, infuriated at the loss. It had taken him years to break in the soft supple leather that flapped comfortably on his hip, lending him the coveted Bohemian professor look he favored. The thieves would be sorely disappointed to find only an assortment of papers and notes for his current lecture series inside. All of which were backed up on his computer at the office. No real loss to speak of, other than the broken window. He walked around to the driver's side to open the door when he was suddenly slammed against the car. A ring of steel pressed into his side.

"Make a sound and you're dead," a voice growled in his ear.

Rough hands patted his pockets and someone yanked out his wallet. Seconds later, he was released from his assailant's grip and shoved to the curb. He glanced over his shoulder in time to see a hooded figure sprint off around the corner. He wasn't in any shape to pursue him—not that he would dare to. He groaned, clutching his hip where he'd collided with the curb. At least the thief hadn't taken his phone. As he staggered to his feet, a police cruiser pulled up alongside him. A young, clean-shaven cop jumped out, reaching out a hand to steady him. "Have you been drinking, sir?"

Andrew gave a disbelieving laugh. "Are you serious? I just got jumped." He pointed to the smashed window. "Someone broke into my car and stole my briefcase. I was only gone for a few minutes. When I got back, some guy pulled a gun on me and made off with my wallet. I don't know if it was the same person."

"Did you get a good look at him?"

"Not really. He was wearing a hoodie."

The cop gave a vacant nod, as though he'd expected as much. "If you want to make a report, the station's just around the corner."

Andrew raised his brows. "Are you even going to follow up on it if I can't identify the guy?"

The cop's expression remained impassive. "He'll toss your wallet once he's emptied it. We might be able to return your driver's license, if nothing else."

Andrew gave a glum nod. "Fine. I'll follow you there."

He pulled into the station parking lot a few minutes later and parked as close as possible to the main door. Judging by the barbed wire and graffiti around the perimeter, he doubted his car would be much safer here than on the street. With as much luck as he was having, he might come back to find another window smashed.

He trudged inside the station and walked over to the officer who was waiting for him in the foyer.

The cop stuck out his hand. "I'm Officer Alvarez."

"Andrew Golding." He gave a wry grin. "Although, currently, I have no way of proving that."

He followed Alvarez into a small office and sat down at the desk.

"Can I get you something to drink?" the officer asked. "Coffee, water?"

"Water would be great, thanks."

Alvarez nodded. "Be right back."

Andrew's phone rang and he dug it out of his coat to see Sage's face on the screen. No doubt, she was checking to make sure he'd gotten rid of the bloody clothing. He'd have to make this quick. Alvarez could reappear at any minute. He tapped the screen and pressed the phone to his ear.

"Raven was just here," Sage blurted out. "She took the urn!"

A prickling sensation broke out on the back of his neck. "Did you get a sample?"

"No! She showed up right after you left. How did she know the urn was here? She's furious about the affair. What if she did something to Jemma? She's so angry with us—maybe she's behind this stunt to frame us."

Andrew frowned, scratching his forehead. "Why would she take the urn back if she planted it?"

"I'm not sure. She said she was going to turn it over to the police."

"One water coming up," Officer Alvarez announced, breezing through the door.

"I've got to go," Andrew muttered into the phone. "I'll

talk to you later." He ended the call, silencing Sage's protests.

"Everything all right?" Alvarez asked, sinking into his chair with a whoosh.

Andrew gave a sheepish shrug. "Just filling my wife in on what happened." He reached for the water bottle and drained half of it in one go.

Alvarez pulled his keyboard toward him and started tapping away on it. "All right, let's start with first and last name."

Andrew's eyes glazed over as he rattled off the requisite details, including his Social Security number and driver's license. He didn't have much faith in anything coming of the report, and he was eager to make a speedy exit. He had bigger problems that needed his immediate attention.

When Alvarez was done filling out the report, he got to his feet. "I sent it to the printer. I'll fetch you a copy for your records." He pointed to Andrew's empty water bottle. "Want another one?"

He shook his head. "I'm good, thanks."

Fifteen minutes went by, before Alvarez finally returned with another officer in tow.

Andrew got to his feet, trying to curb his irritation at the delay.

Alvarez placed the report on the table and tapped a finger on it. "Andrew Golding, professor of medieval literature at Cumbria?"

Andrew flashed him a consummate smile. It was always rewarding when people recognized him. Maybe Alvarez had a kid in his class. "The very same."

"You're under arrest in the disappearance of Jemma Knight."

16

RAVEN

The police had taken her seriously. What choice did they have when she had marched into the station with an urn full of ashes found at her mother's thrift store, and shown them multiple photos of her father consorting with the missing girl? After taking her statement, they assured her they would bring him in for questioning—vindicating her suspicion that he was involved in Jemma's disappearance. Maybe both her parents were. Her mother claimed she had asked Andrew to move out, but Raven didn't trust anything that came out of her mouth either. How could she when she'd been hiding such a checkered past?

She pulled into the Baumgartners' garage and switched off her engine. With her visit to the police out of the way, it was time to do something about Nikki. After doing some cyber snooping, she knew where the girl lived and went to school, but little else about her life. Nothing a little stalking on social media wouldn't rectify. She made herself a latte using the highfalutin espresso machine in the kitchen, then opened up her laptop. As she lifted her mug to her lips, her phone rang. When her mother's number came up, she groaned and slid an irritated finger across the screen. "If you're calling to beg me to reconsider going to the police, you're at least an hour too late."

"Your father's been arrested."

"Glad to hear it. Anything else I can do for you?"

There was a heartbeat of silence before her mother spoke again. "Did you ... give them the urn?"

"What do you think? Of course I did! I may be the spawn of heartless killers, but I'm not a monster."

"Stop ranting, Raven! You know perfectly well we had nothing to do with that girl's disappearance."

"No, I don't! And, by the way, *that girl*'s name is Jemma Knight. What I do know is that you were trying to hide evidence. How sick is that? How would you feel if I went missing? Wouldn't you want people to do everything they could to help the police find my killer?"

"You knew I was planning to take the ashes to a lab this afternoon. I'll go to the police if it turns out to be someone's remains. But if this is just a spoof Jemma has concocted, then you've put your father in a very difficult position."

"No, Mother! Andrew put *himself* in a difficult position, and he put me in an impossible one."

"Stop calling him that! He didn't hurt that girl."

"Someone did. I suggest you let the police do their job and find them. You should get back to figuring out how you're going to get out of the mess you're in."

"You've made things ten times worse for me as well. The police are coming to the store to interview me."

"If you haven't done anything wrong, then you have nothing to worry about."

Her mother let out a weary sigh. "Someone is targeting our family. Please come home, Raven. We need to fight this together."

She frowned down at her mug. "That's not going to happen."

"I can't bear to think of you sleeping rough with those down-and-out friends of yours, or couch surfing at some druggie's place. You're going to end up another street statistic. It's only a matter of time."

Raven smirked to herself as she glanced around the luxurious chef-inspired kitchen with statement fixtures, cathedral ceilings, and steel chandeliers dangling from exposed beams. "I think I'll make it."

"But you—" Sage suddenly sucked in a sharp breath. "Someone's at the door. I've got to go."

Raven set her phone back down on the counter and drained her latte, before turning her attention back to her laptop to browse Nikki Patterson's social media accounts. She searched Facebook first but couldn't find any trace of her. Next, she opened up Instagram. It didn't take long to locate her account—insipid and uninspired with a measly fifty-eight followers. It hadn't been updated in over six months. Raven scrolled quickly back through the posts. Random nature shots, close-up pictures of plates of carb-laden food, and a handful of photos of Nikki flaunting umbrella-festooned drinks with some misfit friends. Nothing of interest, nothing incriminating either.

Frustrated, Raven gave up and started scrolling through her own feed, stopping here and there to read an update from a friend, or respond to the occasional direct message. Just as her eyes were beginning to glaze over, she spotted a post from Thrifty Tails. Her jaw dropped open. A beaming

Nikki stood in the thrift store doorway between Sage and Gloria. Raven's eyes traveled down to the caption beneath.

Thrifty Tails welcomes our newest staff member, Nikki Patterson, passionate defender of the environment and purveyor of pre-used fashion. #thrifting #thriftshop #vintage #thriftstorefinds #preloved #thriftedfashion #secondhand.

17

SAGE

Sage's fingers trembled as she opened the front door at Thrifty Tails. She had feigned a migraine and sent Gloria home early so she could close the store in anticipation of a visit from the police. The burly, balding man with projecting eyebrows standing on the front steps flashed a badge at her. "I'm Detective Meehan. We spoke on the phone earlier. Can I come in?"

Sage gave a tight nod, taking care to lock the door behind him, before leading him through to the back office. "Can I get you something to drink?" Her voice shook as she opened the tiny refrigerator and stared blankly at the contents.

"No thanks. I'm good. I just have a few questions for you and then I'll be on my way."

Sage swallowed hard as she closed the refrigerator door and turned to face him. She had been mentally preparing herself for the worst—possibly even to be arrested—but if that was the detective's end goal, he wasn't giving any indication of it.

"Do you mind?" He gestured to the wooden chair facing her desk before settling into it.

Sage slumped into the mismatched chair opposite him. "How long will you hold my husband?"

Meehan pulled out a notebook and flipped through several pages before finding what he was looking for. "As long as we can. But he's lawyered up. As you know, your daughter gave a full statement attesting to your husband's affair with Jemma Knight. She was able to provide photographic evidence of the two of them together in New Jersey on multiple occasions at different locations."

Sage frowned. Had Raven been following Andrew? How long had she known about Jemma?

"When did you become aware that your husband was having an affair with a student, Mrs. Golding?"

"Please, call me Sage." She squeezed her stiff fingers together in her lap. "I have to admit I was clueless until my daughter told me about it a few days ago. I confronted Andrew immediately. He confessed to having a fling with this girl, but he said he'd broken it off with her a week before she disappeared. My husband's not a violent man, Detective. He didn't do anything to that girl." She bit her lip, recalling Raven's reprimand. She should have used Jemma's name. Was it heartless to keep saying *that girl*? Did it make it sound as though she hated her enough to kill her?

Meehan's face remained expressionless as he scribbled something down. "Where did you discover the urn?"

"Out back in the donations drop off area."

"I'd like to take a look around out there, if you don't mind."

A nerve twitched in Sage's face. She'd been so flustered at being interrupted by Raven that she hadn't finished going through the rest of the donations. What if Meehan found something in one of the other bags—Jemma's shoes or purse or—"

"Mrs. Golding?"

"Yes, of course." She shoved her chair backward and stood abruptly. "This way."

After switching on the exterior floodlights, she led Meehan out to the back yard and pointed out the various stations. "This is our staging area, and over there by the back wall is where the donations are dropped off." She walked over to the miscellaneous mound of bags and boxes. "The urn was in a cardboard box full of home decor items."

"Where is that box now?"

Sage's heart shot to her throat. She should have thought to ask Nikki that before she left. What if it contained more evidence implicating her in Jemma's disappearance? She knelt down and dug aimlessly around in the pile of stuff. "To tell you the truth, I'm not entirely sure. The new girl I hired found the urn. It freaked her out so much I had to let her go home early. I didn't think to ask her which box it came in."

Meehan looked up sharply. "When did this girl start working for you?"

Sage passed a hand over her brow, suddenly feeling overwhelmed. "It was only her second day on the job. I feel terrible about it being so traumatic for her."

Detective Meehan frowned. "I'm going to need her name and contact info."

Sage gave an absentminded nod as she patted her pocket. "I left my phone in the office. I can get that information for you when we go back inside."

Meehan cast a keen eye around the courtyard. "I take it anyone leaving donations would park out here?"

She nodded. "Drop off is between 10:00 a.m. and 3:00 p.m., Monday through Friday."

"Do you have cameras monitoring this area?"

"No, although I've been talking about investing in some —more for my staff's security than anything else. It's not as if we have any high value items in the store."

Meehan bent over and sifted through the contents of a couple of bags and boxes. "Do you know if any other items were dropped off at the same time as the urn?"

Sage looked away, certain her eyes would betray her—that he would see Jemma's bloody clothing reflected in them. She cleared her throat. "There's no real way of knowing that without a camera."

Detective Meehan gave a disappointed nod. His phone beeped and he glanced at the screen. "Excuse me one minute. I need to take this call."

He walked over to the parking area, conversing quietly with someone.

Sage plunged her hands into her pockets, shivering in the late afternoon breeze. It was a relief that Meehan hadn't searched through the rest of the donations. She needed to jump on that the minute he left to make sure there were no other unwanted surprises lurking in the pile.

After a few minutes, he pocketed his phone and strode back over to her. "That was the station. The urn contains concrete mix."

18

SAGE

Sage swayed back on her heels, a flash flood of relief carving its way through her brain. Jemma was alive! Andrew was right— she'd staged the whole thing to punish him for breaking up with her. If only Raven hadn't been so rash, they might have been able to keep the affair under wraps. Andrew could have held on to his job. The mortgage would still be paid. But it was too late now. The damage was done. It was only a matter of time before word got out that Cumbria's beloved professor of Medieval English literature had been writing his own lurid Canterbury Tale with the missing student.

Sage heaved out a juddering breath. "Will my husband be released now?"

Meehan rubbed his jaw, eying her appraisingly. "Already in process. He's cooperating fully with the investigation. At this point, we have no evidence that a crime has been committed, but we've asked him not to leave town without notifying us."

Sage chewed on her lip. In other words, he was still a person of interest in Jemma Knight's disappearance. It wasn't ideal, but it was a whole lot better than being indicted for murder.

"My husband thinks Jemma might be pulling this stunt to get back at him for breaking up with her," she said.

Meehan frowned. "We're not ruling out anything, at this point. But it's a convenient theory if your husband has something to hide."

Sage blinked, taken aback by the detective's candor. He was probing, gauging her response. It wasn't as if she hadn't had the same thoughts herself. But it made it terrifyingly real to hear it coming from Meehan's mouth. Not to mention the fact that it brought back unwelcome memories from another interrogation.

"I've seen enough out here, for now," he said, adjusting his belt. "I'll need that contact info for your staff member before I go."

Her legs felt like elastic beneath her as she led him back inside and pulled up Nikki's file. She wasn't sure why he needed to talk to her, given the fact that the urn had only contained concrete mix, but she supposed it was a matter of tying up loose ends to complete his report.

Meehan passed her his card. "Let me know right away if you get any other unusual donations. And you might want to see about getting a camera installed out back."

Sage accompanied him to the front door and locked it behind him. She needed a few minutes to herself to let the adrenaline subside before heading home to face Andrew. No doubt, he would be reeling from the arrest, indignant about the interrogation he'd endured, craving sympathy. But she wasn't in the right frame of mind to bolster his mood. He had brought this on himself. She had enough of her own problems, and she was carrying that burden alone.

She was locking up the store when her phone rang. Her

heart jumped when Marina's name lit up the screen. *At last!* She hurried into the office and closed the door behind her to take the call, even though there was no one else here. Maybe, now, she would get the answers she needed, but it would be a delicate conversation—she had to proceed with caution.

"Hi, Marina. I didn't know if I'd hear back from you. I thought you might have gotten a new number." Her tone was not unfriendly, but respectably distant. The Marina she had known was a druggie—unpredictable and volatile. Sage wasn't sure how she was going to react to the message she'd left for her. It had been deliberately vague—something about wanting to mend bridges.

"Sorry I'm just getting back to you now," Marina replied in a cheery tone. "My husband and I were in Italy for our ten-year wedding anniversary."

Sage stared at the overflowing shelves in front of her, as stunned as if she'd just been clocked on the side of the head. "You're ... married?"

Marina laughed. "Yes. Does that surprise you?"

It didn't only surprise her—it shocked her. Marina had been hard core into the drug scene and all the wrong people back in high school. It was a miracle she'd survived, let alone go on to lead a normal life.

"Congratulations! I'm ... happy for you," Sage stammered. "Do you have kids?"

"Two girls. Eight and eleven. How about you?"

"I have a twenty-year-old daughter."

"Married?"

Sage's stomach knotted. *Barely*. She clutched the phone a little tighter. "Yes. Going on twenty-two years."

"Sounds like we both made a break for a better life. I got myself into rehab after high school."

"That's fantastic." Sage hesitated, unsure of how to proceed. She had expected to find herself talking to a combative Marina, intent on dredging up past offenses. The person she was speaking with sounded like a well-rounded, happily married woman. Someone she might actually want to be friends with, again. It didn't make sense that Marina was the person who was blackmailing her.

Sage cleared her throat. "I wasn't sure how you'd feel about me reaching out, you know, after what happened."

Marina snorted a laugh. "I don't have any ill feeling toward you, if that's what you're getting at. Trust me, you did me a favor. Taking Jared Brogan off my hands was the best thing you could have done for me. That was the start of me getting clean. And I'm glad you contacted me. It's great to hear from you after all this time. We should get together for coffee and catch up."

Sage wet her lips. "I'd like that. But there's something I wanted to talk to you about. I need this to stay between us."

Marina sucked in a hard breath. "Please don't tell me you're using again."

"No! Never! But it's connected to our past. I'm being blackmailed. Someone's threatening to out me as the snitch who turned Jared in to the cops. To be honest, I wondered if you might have been behind it. Now that I'm talking to you, I realize how ridiculous that sounds, but—"

"But I threatened to!" Marina finished the sentence for her. "I get why you thought it might have been me. I can assure you it's not. That sounds scary. What are you going to do about it?"

"I don't know. I can't go to the police—I'd be putting my family in danger. I've already sent the blackmailer over $30,000. I need to figure out who's behind it before we're bankrupt. Can you think of anyone else in our circle back then who might be desperate enough for money to pull a stunt like this?"

Sage fidgeted in the protracted silence that followed. "Any ideas?" she prompted.

Marina let out a weighty sigh. "I take it you haven't heard—Jared got out on parole a few weeks ago."

19

SAGE

The hair on the back of Sage's neck prickled. Jared a free man—how was that possible? She did a quick calculation in her head. That meant he had been released over a decade early. Her hand shook as she pressed the phone tight to her ear. Her eyes darted around the small office space, probing every corner, imagining his face leering out at her from every nook and cranny. Was it possible it was Jared who was blackmailing her? How had he found out that she was the informant? Likely a process of elimination. He'd had three decades of concentrated time to figure it out.

"Sage? Are you still there?" Marina asked.

"Yes. Just trying to take it in. Are you sure he's been released?"

"Positive. A friend of mine bumped into his mother. She said he had moved back in with her. She's still living in the same house all these years later."

Sage breathed slowly in and out, trying to wrap her head around the idea that Jared Brogan might be back in her life. And not for a good reason. As terrified as she was at the thought of encountering him again, the fire in her belly would not let her run from him this time. She wasn't his to control anymore. He was not going to get away with this. The money she'd already paid him was as good as gone, but she could put an end to his demands for more. She could have him thrown back behind bars in a heartbeat for violating the terms of his parole. She had outplayed him once—she would do it again. The power was in her hands.

"Marina, I have to talk to him. The blackmail demands started right around the time he was released. I need to put a halt to this insanity."

"You might want to rethink that," Marina answered. "Odds are he's even more dangerous after spending thirty years in the can stewing on what he thinks you did."

"I'll stop by his mother's house and talk to him there. He won't try anything stupid in front of her. I can't imagine he wants to go back to prison."

"Do you want me to go with you?" Marina asked, her tone suggesting she had her fingers crossed hoping the answer would be no. Sage had no intention of involving her in this mess. Marina had two young daughters. If there was even the slightest chance Jared would become violent, she couldn't expose her to the risk.

"I'd rather go alone. I don't want him to think we're ganging up on him. I still have his mom's number. If he agrees to meet, I'll tell him I know he's been blackmailing me and give him an ultimatum. If he refuses to quit, or won't admit to it, I'll have no choice but to go to the police with the texts and messages and ask them to investigate him."

"Don't go inside the house unless you know for sure his mother's there. You shouldn't be alone with him, even for a minute."

"Don't worry. I won't put myself in a vulnerable position."

"I don't agree with what you're doing, but it sounds like you're determined to go ahead with it," Marina said. "If you change your mind about needing company, call me."

Sage hung up and slipped her phone into her purse. She hadn't wanted to involve Marina in a situation that could potentially turn hostile, but she didn't relish meeting Jared on her own either. Maybe she could talk Raven into coming with her—that's if she'd even respond to her message. It was worth a try. Sage dialed her daughter's number, shocked when she answered on the first ring.

"Why didn't you tell me Nikki Patterson was working for you?" Raven yelled into the phone.

"Whoa! Take it easy! I mentioned I had a new assistant. I don't remember if I told you her name or not. She said she went to high school with you. Is that a problem?"

"Yes, it's a problem. That girl's had it in for me for years. She thinks I stole the Cumbria Fellows Scholarship from her."

Sage scrunched her eyes shut. What were the odds that the girl she'd hired would turn out to be Raven's high school arch enemy? Was her daughter going to demand she fire Nikki? She couldn't afford to lose another assistant—not even one who wimped out at spiders. She didn't have the energy anymore to sort through all the donations herself. Her symptoms were worsening on an almost daily basis. She inhaled a deep breath, willing herself to react calmly. "That's unfortunate, but I think she's gotten over it by now. She didn't seem unduly interested in you, and she hasn't said a bad word against you. She'd hardly have taken the job, if she still harbored a grudge."

"Are you *seriously* that naive? That's exactly why she took the job! So she could have unlimited access to my family. She's probably the one who's blackmailing you, Mom."

Sage grimaced. "I don't know how you came up with such a far-fetched idea. I'm pretty sure the person who's blackmailing me is the same person I put in prison years ago—Jared Brogan. My loser drug-dealing boyfriend as you dubbed him."

"How do you know that?"

"A friend of mine from high school told me he got out on parole a few weeks back. It can't be a coincidence that, all of a sudden, I'm being blackmailed by someone claiming I snitched to the police."

"But you don't have any proof it's him, do you?" Raven persisted.

"Not yet. I'm working on it. What makes you think it might be Nikki Patterson?"

"Because she's blackmailing me."

20

RAVEN

"Mom, did you hear me?"

"Yes, I heard you, Raven. I'm just having a hard time picturing my cat-phobic, climate-conscious thrift store assistant blackmailing my daughter, let alone me. How does she even know about my past? And why is she blackmailing you and me, and not dad? It doesn't add up."

Raven opened her mouth to respond, then closed it again as it dawned on her that her mother would assume Nikki was blackmailing them both for the same reason. Little did she know that Raven had a past of her own to atone for. She was guilty as charged in the Cumbria Fellows Scholarship heist. How was she going to be able to skirt around the issue of what she'd done and still convince her mother that Nikki was behind the blackmail?

She got to her feet and paced across the travertine kitchen floor. "I don't know how she found out about your past, or why she's not blackmailing Dad—maybe he's next on her hit list. Or maybe she's already approached him too, and he's trying to keep a lid on it with everything else that's going on."

"Are you sure it's Nikki who's blackmailing you? Do you have any proof?"

Raven let out a bark of laughter. "Trust me, it's her."

"I don't understand. How could she possibly know about my connection to Jared Brogan?"

Raven frowned, racking her brain for a way to get her mother to focus on the more important issue—which was getting rid of Nikki. She didn't have time for subtle negotiations. "We can figure that out later. But you have to fire her, today. Don't allow her anywhere near your computer. Letting her work at Thrifty Tails is essentially giving her access into our lives."

"Now you're being dramatic. She's majoring in environmental science at Cumbria. I doubt she's going to be able to hack into my computer."

"That's what she told you," Raven scoffed. "But she's not at Cumbria. She's taking classes at a local community college. And she's not studying environmental science either. She was in my computer club at high school. We were both competing for the same cybersecurity scholarship. She knows exactly what she's doing. She's up to no good. You have to get rid of her as soon as possible."

Raven could almost feel the tension between them as a ponderous silence fell. She had the sinking feeling her mother didn't believe her—choosing instead to believe that lying, slick-lipped has-been over her own daughter. But could she blame her? As far as her mother knew, Raven was the real loser—the dropout druggie slumming with questionable people. It was a portrait she had painted herself in painstaking detail.

"You need to listen to what I'm telling you, Mom. Nikki's not the innocent idealist she's pretending to be."

"Fine. I'll have a talk with her," her mother said, at length. "It just doesn't seem plausible, that's all."

Raven clenched her jaw. "What are you saying? Are you accusing me of lying?"

"I'm not accusing you of anything. You two obviously have some history together and it's understandable if—"

"You know what, forget it! I'm trying to help you out of the mess you're in and you're twisting everything around—making me out to be the one with a chip on my shoulder."

Her mom started to say something in response, but Raven hung up without giving her the chance. She threw herself down in a chair and let out an exasperated sigh, dragging her hands through her hair. She should have stuck to her principles—hung her parents out to dry and called it good. All that talk about banding together to fight as a family meant nothing in the end. She was on her own. Maybe it was for the best. She would handle Nikki in her own way. If her smug mother didn't want to believe what was staring her in the face, she would pay for her ignorance in the end. It was her money to lose. But Raven wasn't going to part with her hard-earned dollars as easily. She had taken Nikki down a peg or two in the past, and she could do it again. First, she had a project to complete for her new job. She wasn't about to jeopardize her paycheck for family or foe.

Falling into a familiar rhythm, she worked steadily and efficiently for the next few hours. Confronting cyber challenges gave her the thrill she needed to break up the monotony of everyday life. Figuring out how to build the type of security architecture that would shield her client from a data breach engaged all the gears of her mind and gave her a kind of runner's high—a much-needed distraction from her personal problems.

She was deep in thought, developing a strategy to secure the processing and storing of her client's sensitive data, when her phone began to ring. She studiously ignored it, eyes riveted on her laptop as she tapped away in a brainstorming frenzy. When she was in the zone, she allowed nothing or no one to pull her out of it. She let the call go to voicemail but, almost immediately, it started ringing again. When it buzzed for a third time, she finally extricated herself from her project and glanced at the screen. *Andrew*. She thought she'd made it clear she didn't want to talk to him. Apparently, not clear enough.

"I'm busy. What do you want?" she snapped into the phone.

"How could you, Raven? You sold me out. I told you I didn't harm Jemma."

"I thought you were only allowed to call your attorney," she scoffed. "Or is that just Hollywood dramatizing the privations of the process? How are you liking your new bracelets, *Andrew*?"

"Quit calling me that. Like it or not, I'm still your father, and I'm not in handcuffs—no thanks to you, I might add. That pot you brought to the police station contained commonplace concrete mix. You threw me under the bus for nothing. Someone is trying to frame our family for murder, and you played right into their hands."

21

ANDREW

Andrew curled his fingers tightly around the steering wheel as he drove to the coffee shop where he and Raven had arranged to meet. He'd had to fight to disguise his shock when she'd agreed to the rendezvous. He hadn't set eyes on his daughter in over a month—although, it turned out she must have had eyes on him on more than one occasion. She had sounded shaken when he told her the urn didn't contain Jemma's ashes. She'd been so sure he had killed the girl, but nothing could be further from the truth. He would never harm Jemma. For all his faults, he wasn't a violent man. He shrank from conflict, which is probably why his marriage was in the state it was in. If he'd had the guts to tell Sage how much he really needed her, and how desperately he missed her when she was off giving speeches and orchestrating animal rights events, they might have found themselves in a healthier place in their marriage. Instead, they had drifted so far apart, he doubted they could ever find their way back to safe harbor.

He pulled into the strip mall parking and made his way to The Brew Parlor, a nondescript coffee shop in an area not frequented by students. The last thing he wanted to have to do was play the role of the gregarious professor doling out scintillating verbal humor on cue. He had nothing left to give of that celebrated persona. He felt unclean, an object of derision, hollowed out by the interrogation he had been subjected to. He had never even set foot inside a police station before making the theft report in East New York. From one minute to the next, he had become the primary person of interest in the disappearance of his student. Thanks to his daughter's rash actions, he had been handled with as much suspicion as a disease-carrying pathogen. It wasn't the kind of attention he was used to, and it stung in all the wrong ways.

After picking up his order at the counter, he slid into a vinyl booth with his paper cup of drip coffee and stared down at it, unable to drum up the will to drink it. Every so often, he cast a skittish glance at the doorway, like a criminal waiting on his counterpart to make an appearance in a B-rated gangster movie. Raven was running late. Would she even show up? Or was this another one of her mind games? He felt like a sitting duck, biding his time until a local media station burst through the door and stuck a microphone in his face. He wouldn't put it past Raven to set him up in such a manner. The lure of financial reward to a druggie knew no bounds.

He startled when she suddenly slid into the seat opposite him. She folded her arms on the table in front of her and pinned a neutral gaze on him. He was pleasantly surprised to see that she still looked like the daughter he knew and loved. Sage was convinced she was doing drugs, but he wasn't so sure about that now that he got a good look at her. Her eyes were clear and focused, and she appeared to be well-groomed, despite the shapeless garb she was dressed in.

He gave her a tentative smile, trying not to appear overly elated at her presence. "What do you want to drink? I'll get it for you."

"Why? Do you think I can't afford it?" She arched a condescending brow before jumping to her feet.

He watched her saunter over to the counter and place an order. He didn't understand her anymore. They used to banter with ease, enjoying each other's sharp-witted exchanges. Now, she wielded words as a weapon against him, jabbing, jousting, pushing him away. She was a lot like her mother in that regard. They were both strong women who made it clear they didn't need his protection or approval. Maybe that was why he had gravitated to Jemma—someone to lionize him, a hero-worshipping groupie. Was he really that pathetic?

Raven resumed her seat, setting a latte and two pastries on the table in front of her. "You might not be homeless, but you looked hungry."

Andrew raised his brows, surprised at how much she was willing to shell out on what had to be a splurge given her current living situation. He and Sage had cut her allowance when she'd dropped out of college—one of the few unanimous decisions they had made of late. "You shouldn't be spending your money on me."

"Why not? You need it more than me. The panhandling business is booming, but I hear criminal lawyers cost an arm and a leg." Raven smirked as she reached for a chocolate croissant.

He gave a sheepish shrug. "I have to admit, you look surprisingly well, all things considered. I didn't know what to expect—you know, hanging out with the unwashed masses and all that."

"Let me put you out of your misery. I took a shower before I came. I didn't want you passing out from street odor."

Andrew gave an approving nod. "Where are you living?"

Raven grinned, munching on her croissant. She carefully wiped her lips on a napkin, rescuing a few flakes of pastry and popping them in her mouth. "Here and there. But we're not here to talk about me."

He dropped his gaze to his coffee cup once more as reality closed in on him like a dark cloud. "I told you that urn was a stupid stunt by Jemma to get back at me."

Raven pushed her plate to one side. "You're partly right. It was a stunt. But it wasn't stupid, and Jemma wasn't behind it."

He threw her an alarmed look. "You don't think your mother—"

"No! She's being targeted too."

"What do you mean *targeted*?"

Raven swallowed a mouthful of coffee. "She's being blackmailed. We both are."

His jaw dropped open. "By Jemma?"

Raven groaned. "No, *Andrew*. This has nothing to do with your missing girlfriend, at least, not directly. Mom hired a new assistant recently. Her name is Nikki Patterson. We were at high school together. She's had it in for me ever since I won the scholarship to Cumbria. She was my only serious competition. She's got it into her head that I cheated, and she's been nursing a grudge against me. She's a nutcase —she was unhinged even back in high school."

"How do you know she's blackmailing you?"

"She confronted me to my face, demanded money to

keep her mouth shut. She's threatening to destroy my career."

Andrew rubbed his jaw. "Why don't you go to the police?"

Raven gave a derisive laugh. "It's not that simple. There are things you don't know about the past—things about Mom."

He drew his brows together in confusion. "What are you talking about?"

"I accidentally found the blackmail messages on Mom's computer. I did some digging around online and discovered she had a boyfriend in high school who was a drug dealer. His name was Jared Brogan. She ratted him out to the police and he ended up getting forty years for a drug-related murder. Other than the cops, no one knew who the snitch was, at least not until now."

A knot tightened in Andrew's stomach. Sage had never as much as hinted at any past involvement with drugs, let alone a drug-dealing boyfriend. Had she been too ashamed to tell him? It wouldn't have changed how he felt about her.

"Nikki's threatening to expose her if she doesn't pay up," Raven went on. "I think she took the job to get close to us—she might even have planted the urn. She was probably planning on blackmailing you next."

Andrew shook his head. "I don't know. This isn't making sense. If no one knew who the snitch was, how did Nikki find out?"

Raven shrugged. "She has skills, I'll give her that. She could have hacked into the police records, or maybe she put two and two together. Either way, she's out to hurt me. Destroying my family is one way of doing it."

"Why doesn't your mother fire her?"

"She doesn't believe Nikki's the one who's blackmailing her."

"Who does she think is behind it?"

"Jared Brogan." Raven shot a quick glance over her shoulder, then lowered her voice. "He was released from prison a few weeks back."

22

ANDREW

Andrew stared at his daughter, goosebumps pricking his arms and spreading across the back of his neck. A thousand different thoughts catapulted through his brain, fighting for purchase. He hadn't known that Sage had a boyfriend who had gone to prison, thanks in part to her role as an informant. And now he was back out on the streets. Was she in danger? Would he come after her, or her family? What if he already had? Was that who had ambushed him in East New York and stolen his wallet? His chest tightened so much he could barely breathe. What if Jared Brogan had killed Jemma, mistaking her for their daughter? A low moan escaped his lips. He would do anything to turn back the clock on his decisions. But that was the insidious thing about time. It only marched in one direction.

"Do you know if your mother has been in contact with this Jared guy?" he asked.

Raven shook her head. "I don't think so. A friend of hers from high school told her he'd been released from prison recently—right around the time she received the first demand for money. That's why she thinks he's the one who's been blackmailing her. She's already sent over $30,000 to an anonymous bank account."

"Are you serious?" Andrew plunged his hands into his hair. He was having a hard time processing everything Raven was dumping on him. It appeared his wife had been in a world of hurt of her own, even before his affair had come to light. No wonder she looked so worn out—defeated, almost—of late.

He pressed his fingers to his temples, trying to clear his thoughts. Whoever was behind the blackmail demands, they had to be stopped before he and Sage were forced into bankruptcy. It wasn't as if they were rolling in cash to begin with. Where was Sage getting the money from to pay the demands anyway? It could hardly be from the thrift store, but he hadn't noticed any large withdrawals from their accounts. She must be using personal credit cards he knew nothing about. His shoulders sagged. They had both been living a lie—past and present.

"Raven, I need you to come with me to convince your mother to go to the police."

She toyed with her coffee cup. "I don't think that's a good idea. The last thing you want is to have the police sniffing around more than they already are. You're not off the hook, yet, when it comes to Jemma's disappearance. What if they think you hired Jared to kill Jemma, and the so-called blackmail money was actually payments to a hitman? The cops are going to home in on you—you're already on their radar. What we need to do is convince Mom to fire Nikki. If we can remove her from our lives, we might be able to eliminate the problem. The likelihood is that Jared Brogan has moved on, and all this has nothing to do with him."

Andrew reached for his lukewarm coffee, finally raising

it to his lips. Raven had a point. Would the police even believe their story? Or would they think someone in the Golding family had hired Sage's ex—a convicted felon—to dispose of their problem? Thirty thousand dollars was a considerable sum of money to hand over to an anonymous blackmailer. Absentmindedly, he reached for the pastry in front of him and broke off a hunk. The sugar melted in his mouth, sweet relief from his problems, but only a temporary hit. The minute he walked out of here, he would be walking into a world of worry. Everything was crashing down around him.

He swallowed his pastry with a swish of coffee. "All right, plan B. Convince your mother to fire Nikki Patterson."

"I told you I tried that already. She won't listen to me."

"Maybe she'll listen to both of us."

He held his breath as he waited for Raven's response. He needed her on board. Sage was desperate to have her daughter back in their lives. Surely, she would take Raven seriously if he backed her up.

"Fine," she said slapping her palms down on the table. " I'll give it one more shot. But if she won't fire her, I'm going to deal with Nikki Patterson on my own terms."

"What does that mean?" Andrew asked, his voice rising in alarm. "Nothing illegal, I trust."

Raven shrugged as she got to her feet. "Define illegal. I'll see you at the house in a few minutes."

"I have to gas up on the way. Go ahead in. Your mom will be happy to see you."

As he drove, Andrew mulled over their conversation. It had come as a complete shock to learn about Sage's past. He couldn't imagine her ever consorting with someone who dealt drugs. When they'd first met, she'd presented herself as a squeaky-clean idealist, passionate about animal rights. She'd only agreed to marry him after making him promise that her dog, Gigi, would be featured in their wedding ceremony. When Gigi died at the ripe old age of twelve, she had sobbed for three weeks straight. It didn't jive with this new rendition of a woman ensconced in the drug scene, dating a man who had murdered someone.

He pulled into a gas station, just as his phone rang. He grimaced when he saw the number lighting up his screen. The academic dean of the English department was hardly calling him with good news. *Let the games begin.*

"Hey, John. What's up?"

The dean cleared his throat. "Andrew, I'm not going to beat around the bush. I've received an anonymous email stating that you were seen with Jemma Knight in New Jersey. There are all sorts of rumors flying around campus. I need you to come clean with me about the nature of your relationship with the missing girl."

Andrew scrunched his eyes shut. The truth was already out. He couldn't take back what he'd done. Lying now would only buy him time. "The rumors are true. I had a brief fling with her, but I ended it the week before she went missing. I had nothing to do with her disappearance, John. Of that, I can assure you."

There was a long pause before the dean spoke again. "As you know, our policies prohibit relationships between professors and students. You've clearly violated our school's faculty code of conduct. You leave me with no choice but to initiate disciplinary proceedings."

23

SAGE

Sage went back-and-forth about whether to call Jared's mother, Carol, or to show up uninvited at her house and try to catch Jared unawares. If she called, and he wasn't home, she would be forced to leave a message —which would place the ball firmly in his court. She would be on tenterhooks until he called back, if ever. And if he didn't respond, she would be no further forward in her quest to root out her blackmailer. Better to meet him face-to-face. If she could look him in the eye, she would know for sure if he was telling her the truth or not. A small part of her hoped she was wrong about him. If it turned out to be Nikki Patterson who was blackmailing her, it would be an easier fix. She could simply fire the girl and threaten her with a lawsuit. But she doubted her assessment of her new hire had been so misplaced. Knowing Raven, she was seizing on the opportunity to settle an old score by pinning the blame on Nikki. Her daughter was a lot like herself—not someone you wanted to go up against.

Her mind made up, Sage locked the thrift store and walked out to her car. She would confront Jared tonight and get it over with. She wasn't a seventeen-year-old under his thumb anymore. It was unlikely he would try anything stupid—fresh out of prison and in his mother's house, of all places—but she was no fool. She needed a way to protect herself if things went sideways.

At the nearby animal shelter where she served on the board, she let herself in the front door. The volunteers had already left for the day, and they didn't have the funds to staff the place at night. After taking a few minutes to greet the three rescue dogs penned up in the back, she made her way to the office, and unlocked the cabinet where they kept the veterinary medicine. She filled a tranquilizer syringe, then slipped it into her purse. It wasn't much of a defense weapon, but it was better than nothing. The dose should be more than adequate to immobilize Jared if the need arose.

The dogs howled when they heard her leaving, pulling on her heartstrings. It was hard enough finding volunteers for the day shift at the small, no-kill shelter. No one wanted to spend the night in this crime-ridden part of town. She was tempted to load the dogs up and bring them home with her—maybe she would, now that she was going to be living alone again.

After climbing into her car, she tapped out a quick text to Andrew telling him she had a meeting and would be back late. She was about to hit send when she changed her mind and deleted it. On a whim, she turned off location sharing, too. She wasn't beholden to him anymore. It was time she started acting like he'd already moved out, and she'd moved on.

As she drove, she rehearsed in her head what she was going to say to Jared.

Congratulations on your early release.

My marriage is falling apart so I thought I'd look up an old flame.

I'm here to buy some dope if you're still selling.

None of it sounded even remotely plausible. She had no legitimate reason to contact Jared. The only way forward was to tell him the truth—at least, the part about being blackmailed and not knowing who was behind it. She certainly wasn't going to confess to the fact that she was the informant who had gotten him locked up for murder. She would deny that all the way to her grave to protect her family. There was a zero-tolerance policy for snitches in the world she had inhabited with Jared Brogan.

It was almost seven-thirty p.m. by the time she pulled up outside his mother's house in Northburg Township. There was a light on inside the family room, and several vehicles were parked along the curb. Sage had no idea who they belonged to, but it was safe to assume someone was home. She took a quick calming breath before climbing out and walking up the stone path to the front door, almost tripping over a large crack in the process. The place hadn't aged well. The original sage-green paint on the front door and window frames was faded and peeling. The yard—once Carol's pride and joy—was bereft of any plantings, and the lawn was a patchwork of holes, weeds, and dead spots.

With an air of trepidation, she rang the doorbell and stepped back to wait. A curtain twitched in the family room window. A moment later, the front door opened, and Carol peeked her head out, blinking warily at her. "Yes, can I help you?"

Sage flashed her a smile to put her at ease. "Carol, it's me, Sage Barker. I was Jared's girlfriend in high school."

The woman's eyes widened. "Oh, yes! I recognize you

now. Come on in." She pulled open the door and beckoned her inside.

"Is Jared home?" Sage asked, stepping into the dingy hallway.

"He just went out to pick up some cigarettes. He'll be back in a few minutes."

Carol led her into the family room and sank down onto the couch, patting the spot next to her. "Sit beside me, dear. My hearing isn't the best. This is a pleasant surprise. I didn't expect to see you again. I heard you got married."

"Yes. I'm Sage Golding now. I have a twenty-year-old daughter, Raven."

Carol's eyes clouded over. "I had hoped to be a grandmother by now. Unfortunately, Jared's poor choices changed the trajectory of my life, too."

A flood of guilt washed over Sage. She wondered what Carol would think if she knew Sage had cooperated with the police and informed on her son in return for immunity. Would she hold it against her? Or would she commend her for her courage? She had been only seventeen at the time—eight years Jared's junior. He had manipulated and used her, and if he hadn't been caught, she might have found herself indicted for murder. A shiver ran across her shoulders. She didn't regret what she'd done.

As if reading her thoughts, Carol reached over and patted her on the knee. "I'm glad you made something of your life, dear."

Sage's lips froze halfway to a smile when she heard the front door open. Now that the moment had come, she wasn't sure she was ready to face the man she had betrayed.

Would he see guilt written all over her face?

24

SAGE

Sage smoothed out her skirt with shaking hands, holding her breath as Jared's footsteps came ever closer to the room they were sitting in. Then, suddenly, he was looming in front of her, his large frame almost filling the doorway, his rugged, bad-boy good looks roughed up and tattooed from decades behind bars, but instantly recognizable.

She made no attempt to stand. It wasn't as if a dignitary had entered the room—he was a convicted felon. More important, she didn't think her legs would hold her.

"Hello, Jared." Her voice sounded surprisingly calm, at odds with the erratic beat of her heart.

A flicker of surprise shot across his face, but he quickly masked it. "Well, if it isn't Sage Barker." He rubbed his jaw, his gaze traveling unapologetically over her. "What are you doing back in the ghetto? I heard you turned into one of those crackpot animal rights activists."

He pulled off his sweatshirt and settled his muscular frame into the upholstered chair facing her. Arms dangling down the sides, he grinned across at her. He seemed more amused to see her than anything else. Nothing in his expression hinted at any animosity, let alone a burning desire for vengeance. Sage was beginning to regret her rash decision to come here. The last thing she wanted to do was stir up Jared's interest in her unnecessarily. Maybe she should have taken Raven's advice and investigated her new assistant a little further, first.

She cleared her throat. "Marina told me you were out on parole. I was in the neighborhood, so I thought I'd stop by to say *hi*—you know, for old time's sake."

Jared snorted as he reached for the pack of cigarettes in his shirt pocket and pulled one out.

Carol flapped a hand at him. "Not in here, Jared, *please*. We've been over this enough times already. My old lungs can't handle it."

Jared scowled as he lit up a cigarette. "About time you pottered off to bed, Mom. Sage and I have some catching up to do." He winked across at her. "For old time's sake."

"Actually, I can't stay," Sage said, reaching for her purse. "I'm on my way home."

Jared feigned a wounded expression, pressing a hand to his heart. "You just got here. At least have the decency to catch me up on the last thirty years of your life before you disappear on me again."

Carol got to her feet with a grunt. "I'll leave you two to chat. Jared, make the girl a cup of tea. And put out that cigarette."

Sage fidgeted in her seat as Carol shuffled out of the room and closed the door behind her. Now would be a good time for her to make an exit, too, but she was loathe to leave without answers.

Jared took a puff of his cigarette, eying her appraisingly. " Never thought we'd be sitting in this room together again after all this time. How about a drink? I can drum up something a little stronger than tea."

Sage forced a fleeting smile. "Not for me, thanks."

"You never used to make me drink alone." Jared walked over to a small liquor cabinet to the left of the ancient television. "You came all the way here to see me. The least you can do is celebrate my release with me." He filled a shot glass with whiskey and handed it to her, eying her ruefully. "Why did you quit visiting me? You were the only one who stuck by me after I got locked up. Then one day you didn't show up—no message, no excuse, no let-down letter. You just upped and moved on with your life. Found some other guy, got married, had a kid, opened a thrift store, got busy saving the flea-bitten mongrels of New York."

Sage wet her lips with the whisky, then set her glass on the end table. Her hands were shaking too hard to hold it. She hadn't realized Jared had been keeping such close tabs on her all these years. "I was seventeen. I was hardly going to wait for you for forty years. You can't hold that against me."

"Turned out to be only thirty." He raised his shot glass, leering at her. "I don't begrudge you living your life. You're here now and that's all that matters." He drained his glass and immediately refilled it. "Tell me about your husband."

Sage gave an abashed shrug. "There's not much to tell. We're a pretty boring couple leading an ordinary life. He's a professor at Cumbria."

Jared's lips curled into a lewd grin. "Sage Barker didn't used to be boring."

A flush crept up the back of her neck as he continued to ogle her. She didn't want to talk about what she used to be like. Drugs had made her do a lot of brainless things.

Jared threw back another shot of whiskey. "How old's your daughter?"

"She just turned twenty."

"Is she a looker like her mother?" He stepped toward her and pulled her to her feet, ruffling her hair, sniffing it. "Still soft as butter. You smell good, babe."

She gave a nervous laugh and tried to pull away, but his hand slipped behind her back, pressing her to him like a band of steel. He moved to kiss her, but she twisted her head to one side and thumped him on the chest. "Stop it, Jared! What are you doing? I'm married, remember?"

His eyes narrowed, but he released her from his grip. "I thought this was what you wanted. *For old-time's sake*, you said. Why else did you come here?"

Sage took a quick calming breath. "I'm being blackmailed."

A frown cleaved a deep groove between Jared's eyebrows. "Who's behind it?"

She studied his expression but couldn't detect any sign of deception. "I don't know. I was hoping you could help me with that."

He smoothed a hand over his head. "Why are they blackmailing you?"

"It has to do with our past. They blame me for snitching on the drug operation, and getting you arrested for that dealer's murder. At first, I thought Marina Garber might have been behind it, but I talked to her and ruled her out. She went through rehab; she's been clean and sober for years—happily married with two daughters of her own. She's not bearing any grudges against me. Any idea who else it could be?"

"Maybe." Jared worked his jaw side to side, his gaze boring into her. "But first, I have a question for you."

25

RAVEN

Raven frowned when she pulled up outside her parents' place. The house was in darkness. She tried calling her mom's number, but it went straight to voicemail. She tapped her hand impatiently on the steering wheel. Maybe she was working late at the store. With a bit of luck, she had fired Nikki, after all, and was sorting through the donations herself after hours.

She dialed her dad's mobile next. "Hey, Mom's not home yet, and she's not picking up. Can you swing by Thrifty Tails on your way and see if she's there? She might have left her phone in the office and gone out back to sort the drop-offs."

"Will do. Wait for me at the house. The key's where we always keep it."

Raven exited her car and walked around to the back of the house to retrieve the spare key from the garden shed where it had hung for years. She had left her own key to the house next to a scathing note for her parents on the kitchen table when she'd moved out. She cringed when she remembered some of the unhinged things she'd written—dousing her parents with a barrage of hate-filled accusations of hypocrisy and neglect—mostly unfounded. But she'd been hurting inside at the secrets they'd kept from her and each other, and unable to bring herself to confront them. She hoped they'd tossed the letter—preferably, burned it. It wasn't the kind of legacy you could be proud of years down the line.

Inside the house, Raven brewed herself a cup of decaf coffee. She was about to open up her laptop and tackle some work, when it occurred to her that now would be a good time to look for that letter and destroy it. Leaving her coffee cup on the table, she went into the office and began searching. She had no idea where her mother would have stashed something like that—it wasn't the type of memory you saved in a keepsake box.

She worked methodically through the drawers and closets, but there was no sign of the letter, or the key she had returned along with it. Frustrated, she emptied out the stackable letter trays and penholder on the desk, and rummaged through an assortment of paper clips, erasers, and miscellaneous paperwork, but to no avail. As she attempted to put everything back the way she'd found it, her gaze landed on a small notepad sticking out from beneath the keyboard. She pulled it out and spun it around to read what her mother had written.

Carol 212 365-7728

Raven frowned. Off the top of her head, she couldn't think of any Carols in her mom's circle. Probably someone inviting her to speak at an event. The sound of the garage door rolling up sent her scuttling out of the office, and back to the kitchen. She sat down at the table and opened up her laptop.

Moments later, her dad strode into the room. He ran a

hand distractedly through his hair. "Your mother's not at the thrift store."

Raven shrugged. "She's probably off giving one of her talks. We'll just have to wait until she gets back."

Dad sank down in the chair next to her. "I called Gloria to see if she knew anything. She said your mother closed the store early today—blamed it on a migraine, but Gloria didn't believe her. She said she was acting strangely."

Raven furrowed her brow. "That does sound weird. I've never known her to get a migraine."

"She's looking a bit rundown, to be honest. I wish she'd cut back on some of her speaking engagements." Her dad glanced at his watch. "If she's giving a talk, she won't be back for another couple of hours. Want to grab some dinner—my treat?"

Raven closed the lid of her laptop. "So long as we go someplace no one knows us. I don't want the servers giving the villainous professor dirty looks all night."

Her dad frowned. "My name's not out there, yet, although the dean's starting disciplinary proceedings against me, so it won't be long."

"The photos are already making the circuit. Someone other than me was snapping pictures of you and Jemma. It won't be long before some online sleuth puts a name to your mugshot."

Her dad scratched nervously at his neck. "What kind of pictures did you turn over to the police?"

She threw him a look of disgust. "You and Jemma going in and out of coffee shops and restaurants. You don't need to be locking lips for it to be obvious what was going on."

She picked up her laptop and got to her feet. "You can drive, I can't afford gas." Angling her face away, she hid a sneer. She felt justified making his life a little bit more miserable than it already was. She could never forgive him for what he'd done. This was only a temporary truce to get to the bottom of the blackmail.

By the time they got back after dinner, her mother still hadn't shown up, and she wasn't answering her phone.

"Something's not right," Raven said. "Mom never has her phone off this long. Did you notice anything odd at Thrifty Tails? Any indication that she might have left in a hurry?"

Her dad shook his head. "No, can't say I did. Everything was locked up and put away. Although, she did leave her computer on."

Raven's brows shot up. "Was she working on something?"

"I'm not sure. Nikki's employment application was on the screen. I left the computer running in case she was in the middle of something."

A frisson of fear shot through Raven's veins. "She must have been looking into what I told her about Nikki. Maybe she found something. I'm going to go back to the store and take a look. Mom might have gone to Nikki's house to confront her. I'll get the address."

Her dad threw her an alarmed look. "You don't think Nikki would do anything to harm your mom, do you?"

She arched a withering brow. "I wouldn't put it past her. She's bitter to the core."

Her dad reached for his car keys. "I'm coming with you."

"No. You wait here in case Mom comes back. Call me if she shows up."

"You can take my car, if you want."

She rolled her eyes. "I was kidding about the gas."

Her dad blinked, looking disconcerted. "Don't do anything stupid. Your mom might be trying to reason with Nikki in the hope of turning this around without pressing charges. You know what a big heart she has for hurting animals, and this girl sounds like she's hurting."

Raven snorted as she snatched up her purse. "Trust me, she's no wounded animal. Mom's walking into the jaws of a predator."

26

RAVEN

There was a lot more about Nikki Patterson that Raven hadn't shared with her parents. She had terrorized her classmates with her vicious tongue and bullying tactics, but it went far beyond that. Raven was convinced the woman was dangerous, and for good reason. Nikki had been suspected in a case of arson involving a boy she'd had a crush on in high school. She had been harassing his girlfriend for some time: gluing her textbooks together, throwing food at her—she'd even been suspended for a couple of days for punching her. When his car was set alight during prom night, he accused Nikki of being behind it, but it had never been proven.

Raven shivered as she drove, remembering the twisted grin on Nikki's face when she'd threatened to destroy her career if she didn't pay up. She was relentless—fueled by hate and resentment. Hard to know how far she would go to get revenge on anyone who crossed her, or hurt her, but Raven had no doubt she was capable of upping the ante from her high school days.

She had some sympathy for Nikki's position. But the

reality was, she may not have won the scholarship anyway, even if Raven hadn't run interference in retaliation for Nikki deleting her application. In some ways, they were more alike than Raven cared to admit. The difference was that Nikki was festering away on the inside and destroying her life in the process. Her paranoia and insecurity drove her to sacrifice even her own best interests for the sake of getting revenge. This time she'd gone too far.

Raven pulled into the back parking lot at Thrifty Tails and darted a skittish glance around the deserted yard. A mouse scampered by her feet, making her jump. The area was poorly lit. If anyone was waiting in the shadows, she would be an easy target. Gripping her mace spray in one hand, she jumped out of the car and sprinted to the back door. After punching in the entry code, she slammed it shut behind her and locked it, then let out a long, relieved breath. A moment later, she froze. Her gaze landed on a strip of light at the bottom of the door leading into the store. Was her mother here after all? Had Dad missed her when he came by earlier? But where was her car? It wasn't like her to park on some unlit side street.

Raven tip-toed into the darkened office. The computer was in sleep mode but still running, just as her father had left it. She pulled out her phone and dialed her mother's number, listening intently for its distinctive ring coming from inside the store. *Nothing*. Maybe there was no one here at all. Dad could have forgotten to turn the light off. Her heart drummed in her chest like pelting rain as another thought occurred to her. What if Nikki was here? Holding her breath, she padded back out into the hallway and slowly cracked open the door leading into the store. Her eyes zigzagged across the space, widening in surprise when she spotted Gloria pacing behind the register, her phone pressed to her ear. Relief melded with confusion in her brain. What was the store manager doing here at this time of night? She retreated behind the door, and took a few shallow breaths, unsure if she should reveal her presence. She was still debating what to do when Gloria's head suddenly swiveled in her direction. "Who's there?" she called out, an edge of tension in her voice.

Grimacing, Raven pushed the door fully open and stepped into the store. "Hey, Gloria! It's just me, Raven. I came by to pick something up. Didn't know anyone was here."

Gloria quickly pocketed her phone and walked over to her. "You scared me, honey! Is your mom back, yet?"

"No. Dad's at the house waiting on her."

Gloria enveloped her in a hug. "You poor thing. You must be worried sick. I know I am. I came back to check the office calendar in case she had a speaking engagement booked, but there's nothing marked on it for tonight. I've been calling around the animal shelters asking if she was giving a talk somewhere, but no one's aware of any event taking place tonight."

Raven forced her lips into the semblance of a grateful smile. Gloria's explanation didn't ring true. The animal shelters were closed at night—no one was going to answer the phone. But why would Gloria lie to her? What was she really up to? Stealing? That didn't make sense either. If she was pilfering inventory, she could easily do it during the day. There were plenty of times she was left alone in the store. Raven's suspicions were quickly leading her down a more speculative path. Did Gloria come here to meet someone—Nikki, perhaps? Was she involved in blackmailing Mom?

"Your mother seemed a little down this past couple of days." Gloria fixed an anxious gaze on her. "You don't think she'd ... harm herself, do you? It's just that with everything she's dealing with right now, she must be feeling overwhelmed."

Raven averted her gaze, taking a moment to devise a response. How much did Gloria know about what was going on in their family? She knew Raven had dropped out of college and she probably thought she was living with some undesirable friends. But that was as far as it went. Her mother hadn't told anyone about the blackmail—Raven had discovered it inadvertently. Had Sage confided in Gloria about her husband's infidelity? It seemed unlikely, especially given the fact that Jemma Knight was missing. Raven couldn't fall into the trap of divulging anything her mother hadn't elected to share with her employee. She didn't know if she could trust her. Best to play dumb.

She blinked guilelessly at Gloria. "What do you mean?"

Her eyes crinkled with concern. She reached out a hand and laid it on Raven's shoulder. "Oh, honey, you don't know, do you?"

27

ANDREW

For a long time after his daughter left, Andrew remained seated at the kitchen table with his head in his hands. He had screwed up everything. Sage hadn't trusted him enough to tell him she was being blackmailed. And now she was trying to take care of the problem on her own—using credit cards she had no way of paying back. She was playing with fire if she was planning on confronting her blackmailer, whoever it turned out to be. Jared Brogan sounded like a particularly dangerous character—surely she wouldn't be reckless enough to meet up with him on her own. Not that it gave Andrew much peace of mind to think that she might have gone to see Nikki instead. If Raven were to be believed, Nikki Patterson was unhinged. Would she lash out at Sage if she confronted her? He could only hope his wife had managed to persuade her to drop the blackmail threats. His stomach knotted as he considered the alternative. If Sage went missing too, he would become the number one suspect in the disappearance of both his wife and his lover. It was the stuff of a crime show special on steroids.

He leaned back in his chair and rubbed his jaw. There was also the possibility that Sage's disappearance had nothing to do with Nikki Patterson or Jared Brogan. His wife mixed it up with some strange people at times. They'd had their fair share of arguments about it over the years. He should have asked Gloria if she'd noticed any suspicious strangers hanging around the store. He'd always been worried about the kind of clientele the thrift store attracted. Sage called him prejudiced for even entertaining the thought, but she'd been forced to call the police on more than one occasion when a customer had threatened her with a weapon.

He let out a heavy sigh. He was getting way too worked up thinking about worst case scenarios. It was entirely possible there was a simple explanation for Sage's absence. She could have gone out for drinks with friends, or to the movies, or maybe to dinner with some of her animal rights benefactors. It wasn't like she wanted him to know her movements. She'd as good as kicked him out of the house, and she'd made a point of turning off location sharing, as though to signal another cord had been cut.

He checked his phone again but there were still no messages from either Sage or Raven. His thoughts turned to Jemma. As the days went by, he was beginning to doubt her disappearance was merely a stunt to punish him. He felt sick to his stomach picturing all the things that could have happened to her. What if she'd been accosted in the park after he'd left her there, distraught and not thinking rationally? It seemed all he did was inflict pain on the women in his life—including a young woman who should never have been in his life to begin with.

He got up and poured himself a hefty glass of wine. He needed something to take the edge off the guilt coiling around his innards like a boa constrictor. He was trapped in a tower of regret of his own making. He should never have disposed of that bag of bloody clothing. A decent human being would have turned the evidence in and faced the fallout. He quickly drained his glass and refilled it. When the bottle of Cabernet was empty, he tossed it in the recycling and put his glass in the dishwasher. He couldn't sit here feeling sorry for himself any longer. He wasn't the man he wanted to be, but he could do better than drinking himself into oblivion.

He wandered into the office and began rummaging aimlessly. He told himself he was looking for clues as to where Sage might have gone but, in truth, he was trying to comfort himself by soaking up her essence. Tears prickled his eyes. He couldn't envision life without her. She had always been the lioness by his side. He was the life and soul of the party, but she was the rock and the driving force in the family. When she'd first floated the idea of opening a thrift store to support animal causes, he had scoffed at it—said it was beneath her. If he was being honest with himself, he deeply admired her convictions. Why couldn't he simply have told her that? Why did he always act as though his career was all that mattered? Granted, he was paying the mortgage, but she was the one making real change happen in the world. His entertaining lectures would be long forgotten by his graduating students, but her efforts to support a worthy cause would stand the test of time.

Glancing distractedly around the desk, his gaze fell on a small notepad next to the keyboard. He pulled it toward him and read the note scribbled on it.

Carol 212 365-7728

Who was Carol? Another one of her crazy cat rescue circle, no doubt. He tossed the notebook back on the desk and scrubbed his hands over his face. He couldn't stand the silence any longer. He needed to talk to someone. Someone he could trust. Sinking down in the swivel chair at the desk, he dialed Carmen's number.

"Andrew?" She yawned loudly. "Sorry! Everything all right?"

He glanced at his watch and grimaced. It was already quarter after ten at night. No wonder she sounded groggy.

"I shouldn't have called you so late. I didn't know who else to call."

"What's wrong? Is it Sage?"

Andrew frowned. Did Carmen know she was missing?

"Why do you ask?"

There was a long pause before Carmen answered. "I just thought maybe ... you know ... with the diagnosis and all."

Andrew stared blankly at the bookshelves on the wall facing him. His head was spinning from the bottle of wine he had drunk far too quickly. Had he misheard her? "What diagnosis?"

Carmen's tone was subdued. "She promised me she was going to tell you this week. Sage has ALS."

28

ANDREW

Andrew's stomach began to heave. He snatched up the trash can from under the desk and held it beneath his chin, certain he was going to throw up the wine sloshing around in his stomach. ALS was a death sentence. No wonder Sage had been looking so peaked of late. It had never even occurred to him that she was sick—he'd been so consumed with his own issues. After a moment or two, the wave of nausea began to subside, and he set the trash can back down on the floor.

"Andrew? Are you still there?" Carmen asked.

"Yes, I'm here. I'm ... shocked, that's all. Sage didn't say anything about it to me. Things have been difficult between us."

"Is it true?" Carmen asked quietly. "About you and Jemma Knight? Are you the older man she was seen with?"

He exhaled a hot breath. "Yes. We had a fling, nothing more. It was the stupidest thing I've ever done. I ended it the week before she went missing." He let out a groan. "You have to believe me, Carmen. I didn't do anything to hurt that girl."

"I didn't say you did. You sound hysterical. Have you been drinking?"

"Just some wine. I'm out of my mind with worry. Jemma was completely infatuated with me. She took it badly when I broke things off. What if she's harmed herself?"

"That's a quantum leap. Maybe she just needs some time to cool her jets," Carmen answered. "You shattered her fantasy when you ended things with her."

"Believe me, I know—that's why I'm panicking." Andrew let out a shuddering sigh. "It's not just her I'm worried about. Sage hasn't come home tonight."

"Whoa! Is there a medieval abductor in the house?"

"This isn't funny, Carmen, I need someone to believe in me. The dean has begun disciplinary proceedings against me. I'm probably going to end up losing my job over this. But I don't want to go to prison for something I didn't do. I need your help."

"How am I supposed to help you? I teach language, not law."

"You can start by telling me everything you know about Sage's diagnosis. Is it confirmed? How advanced is it? Do you think she would hurt herself? Did she ever talk to you about taking her own life?"

"Okay! Slow down. She just found out about it a couple of weeks ago. They're still running tests. And no, she's not giving up. She was devastated, naturally, but she's a warrior. She's going to fight it—take it on like every other cause she's ever gotten behind. You know what she's like."

Andrew stared down at the hand-poured glass paperweight he'd bought for Sage during a trip to Hawaii for their twenty-year wedding anniversary. Would she still be here to celebrate another one? She'd been wrestling with muscle cramps and insomnia for several months now. He had condescendingly blamed it on the mold in the thrift store—even suggested she sell it.

Understandably, she had clammed up after that. It was only after she'd complained of shortness of breath that she finally went to the doctor. Had he even asked her how her appointment had gone? He frowned, trying to think back. *Yes!* He had brought it up at dinner one night, for lack of anything else to talk about. She had dismissed it, told him everything had checked out fine. She had outright lied to him. She hadn't wanted his support or needed it. Instead, she'd chosen to confide in a mutual friend. It stung, but he didn't deserve to indulge in the rejection. He had brought it on himself.

"How bad is it?" he asked, bracing himself for Carmen's answer.

"I don't know. She's going through some tests right now. After that, her doctors will decide on the best way to manage her symptoms. If anyone can take this on, she can, Andrew. You know what an indomitable spirit she is."

The briny tang of tears prickled his nose. He didn't know if Carmen was only saying that to make him feel better, but he didn't care. It was exactly what he needed to hear. If Sage was going to fight, he would fight alongside her. But first, he had to find her.

"She isn't answering her phone," he said. "I'm not sure if she's ignoring me or if something's wrong. Our marriage has been in a bad place for a long time. She asked me to move out, but I haven't, yet. Maybe not coming home is a form of protest on her part, but it's driving me insane not knowing. Can you try calling her? She might pick up if it's you. I hate to drag you into the middle of this, but I just need to know that she's okay."

"All right. Give me a few minutes. I'll hang up and try her right now."

Andrew got to his feet and plodded back to the kitchen. He brewed himself a strong coffee—sleep was out of the question at this point—then pulled out his phone to message Raven. *Any updates?* He stared at the unsent text for a moment before deleting it. What if she messaged back, asking him the same thing? What would he say in response? *Yes, your mother's dying.* He wasn't about to have that conversation over text. Apparently, Sage hadn't told Raven about her diagnosis either—hardly surprising. They had barely spoken for the past month. They had fallen apart entirely as a family. And now that he wanted to put the pieces back together, Sage was about to be cruelly snatched from them by a diagnosis none of them had seen coming.

His phone rang, startling him out of his dismal reverie.

"She didn't pick up," Carmen said, her ordinarily jovial tone laced with concern.

He squeezed his eyes shut. "Thanks for trying. Let me know right away if she contacts you."

He hung up and rolled his knotted shoulders—weighted down with a new and heavier burden. It wasn't fair to keep Raven in the dark about her mother's diagnosis. She would find out about it at some point. Tonight was as good a time as any.

29

SAGE

Jared blew a puff of smoke in Sage's face. "Was it you who sold me out?"

She shifted her stance, one eye on the door. She should have left when Carol went to bed. The conversation with Jared had taken a precarious turn, catching her off guard.

She forced a laugh, hoping her voice sounded more confident than she felt. "Don't be ridiculous, Jared! Do you seriously think I would have come here if I'd been the one who ratted you out? I'm here because I need your help to figure out who's blackmailing me. I trusted you enough to believe it's not you. You owe me the same amount of faith in return."

"What makes you think I owe you anything? You're the one who walked away from me." Jared folded his arms in front of him, his gaze analytical and probing. "I've had a long time to think things over, and I've eliminated everyone in our circle back then as the snitch. The only person I can't rule out is you."

Mustering her courage, Sage walked over to him,

gripped him by his rock-hard arms, and shook him. "That's exactly what they want you to think, don't you see that? Whoever sold you out is the same person who's blackmailing me. They're trying to frame me. If we can find the blackmailer, you'll find the person who turned you in to the police."

Jared grinned, an ugly grin that felt like it came from somewhere deep inside his dark heart. "You're thinking like a criminal. I like it."

Sage shivered inwardly. He was chomping at the bit to get his hands around the throat of the person who had put him behind bars for the best decades of his life. She had no real intention of enlisting his help to nail the blackmailer. Her only goal now was to get out of this house alive. But she couldn't show the fear pumping through her—it would make her a marked woman. The dynamics of their past relationship had burned abiding pathways through her brain.

After a few tense minutes, Jared's expression relaxed. "I can put a few feelers out. I still have connections." He reached for her hair and twirled a chunk of it around his finger. "What's it worth to you?"

"Don't go there, Jared," she said. "I'm happy you're out, but I'm not going to throw away my family for you."

He chuckled, slowly unraveling her hair in a suggestive manner. "A pompous professor could never satisfy a woman like you."

Averting her gaze, she threw the strap of her purse over her shoulder, and rummaged inside it for a piece of paper, careful not to expose the syringe. "Here's my number," she said, scribbling it down. "Call me if you get any leads."

He took the note from her and stuffed it into the back pocket of his jeans. "You'll owe me if I take care of your problem for you. Might want to start thinking about what my reward's gonna be."

Sage gave a tight-lipped smile as she walked over to the family room door. She was nearly through it when a heavy hand dropped on her shoulder, melding her to the spot. Dread uncurled its talons in her gut. She had almost made it out—*almost*. But she should have known better. Jared thrived on intimidation, toying with people like they were prey. You never knew where you stood with him. He had been in full control in their relationship—until the day she'd ended his reign of terror with a lie that had bought her three decades of freedom from his reach. She spun around to face him, painting a defiant look on her face.

His expression was one of amusement, throwing her for a loop once more. "You didn't say goodbye."

"Goodbye, Jared." She turned on her heel and strode to the front door with all the strength she could drum up. It felt like adrenaline was leaking from her with every step, but she forced herself to keep marching on like a wounded soldier on a battlefield never knowing when the final bullet would take her down. As she exited the house, she glanced over her shoulder to see him leaning against the doorframe, the same cocky smile playing on his lips. Was Jared her blackmailer? He hadn't denied it. He wanted to keep her guessing. Everything was a game to him.

Safely in her car, she locked the doors and drove off into the darkness. If Jared had only realized he'd had the snitch at his fingertips, she'd never have made it out of there alive. Her heart pulsed at the top of her throat, her headlights the only illumination on the country road. The shadowy hedges were so high on either side she could scarcely see beyond them. She'd forgotten what it was like to live outside of the twenty-four-seven lights of the city.

It was late, and she still had an hour's drive back home. Was Andrew wondering where she was by now? Did he even care? She missed her dog now more than ever. Gigi had always been thrilled to see her when she got home, her little body wiggling from head to toe. With Raven gone, and Andrew checked out, home held less appeal than ever. Maybe that was why she availed herself of every invitation to speak. It wasn't only passion that drove her, it was loneliness.

She was digging her phone out to check for messages when she noticed a car behind her flashing its lights. She slowed down and hugged the side of the road to allow them to pass, but the car fell back, continuing to tail her. When they flashed her a second time, she frowned, wondering if she had a flat tire or something. Regardless, she wasn't about to pull over on a dark road at this time of night. She would stop at the next gas station.

When she glanced in her rearview mirror again, the car was suddenly coming up behind her, impossibly fast. A loud, crunching sound filled the air, and her head snapped forward, then backward, sending shockwaves through her entire body. Slamming on the brakes, she sat frozen and disoriented, trying to process what had just happened.

A moment later, the passenger door opened. A surge of fear went through her when she saw the gun pointing at her.

30

RAVEN

Raven pinned a searching gaze on Gloria. Panic swelled in her throat, making it difficult to breathe. "What are you talking about? What don't I know? Why are you looking at me like that?"

Gloria wrung her hands. "It's not my place to tell you, honey. You need to go home and have a conversation with your parents. They miss you dreadfully."

Raven clenched her jaw. *Not that dreadfully.* They had plenty of time for things they were more interested in than their wayward daughter—like Jemma Knight, and rescue animals. "I know Mom asked Dad to move out, if that's what you're getting at."

Gloria blinked at her, a confused look in her eyes. "I ... didn't know that. Where is your father living?"

"At home. He hasn't left yet."

Gloria frowned. "Your dad's never been physical with your mom, has he?"

Raven narrowed her eyes at her. "What are you suggesting? Dad would never do anything to hurt her."

"No, of course not. You're right. It's just strange that she disappeared after she asked him to move out—you know, with his girlfriend disappearing too." She pressed a fist to her lips, then shook her head. "I don't know what I'm saying. It's late, and I'm tired. I need to go home, although I doubt I'll be able to sleep."

"Wait! Before you go, what were you trying to tell me about Mom?"

Gloria smiled sadly at her. "Go home, Raven. Talk to your parents. You won't have them around forever." She walked to the front door and opened it, then called over her shoulder. "Don't forget to turn off the lights and lock up when you're leaving. And be careful. It's not safe around here at night."

Raven watched Gloria amble out to her car and drive off. Why was she being so evasive? She got the feeling Gloria had been lying to her about what she was doing in the store to begin with. Who had she been talking with on the phone? Clearly, she hadn't expected to be interrupted. Raven glanced around—nothing seemed to be out of place. No bags or boxes half-packed up with inventory Gloria had been planning on secreting out of here. Raven doubted the cash register held enough money to be worth stealing. Besides, Gloria had always been a trustworthy employee. She had worked at Thrifty Tails for as long as they'd been open.

As Raven walked back to the office, her phone rang.

"Hey, Dad," she answered, before she could catch herself. *Andrew!* But it was petty to correct herself after it was already out of her mouth.

"Raven, I need you to come home right away."

She frowned at the strained tone in his voice. "Why? Is Mom back?"

He hesitated. “No, not yet. But I need to talk to you about something.”

“I’m not done here.”

“It can wait. This is important.”

“More important than trying to find Mom? What’s going on? Are you being arrested again?”

Her dad sighed. “No. But we need to talk.”

She tried to curb her irritation. “Go ahead. I’m listening.”

“It’s not something I want to discuss over the phone.”

She let out an exasperated groan. ”I’m sick and tired of the mind games you and Mom play. Can you at least tell me what it’s about?”

“It’s about Mom. There’s something I need to tell you—in person.”

Raven fell silent, Gloria’s words coming back to mind. *Oh honey, you don’t know, do you?* Fear slithered around her throat, choking off her air supply once more. She wasn’t sure she wanted to hear what her father had to say. Not if it was something worse than being blackmailed, worse than her parents’ marriage falling apart, worse than her father losing his career over the stupid decision he’d made to sleep with a student.

She closed her eyes, weighing his words. She couldn’t face any more bad news at the moment. She needed to stay focused on the task at hand. “I’ll be back soon. We can talk about it then. First, I need to pay Nikki Patterson a visit and find out if that’s where Mom went.”

She hung up before he could argue with her. In the back office, she settled down in front of the ancient computer and began reading through Nikki’s employment application. Within seconds, she had all the information she needed downloaded to her phone. She couldn’t wait to see the look on Nikki's face when she showed up unannounced at her house—returning the favor. Only this time, she would be the aggressor.

Nikki Patterson was not going to get away with terrorizing her family like she'd terrorized everyone at school. Raven grinned to herself as she turned out the lights and locked up the thrift store.

Nikki needed to be taught another lesson, and Raven was more than qualified for the job.

31

RAVEN

Raven unwrapped a piece of gum and stuck it in her mouth, before plugging in her phone and firing up her GPS. She grimaced when she saw that the drive time was almost fifty minutes. Her mother should have thought to question why a part-time, minimum-wage employee would drive so far to work when there had to be hundreds of thrift stores closer to where she lived. Her bleeding-heart mother was too prone to believe the best of everybody. Raven would have flagged that anomaly from the outset. Good detective work was a prerequisite for the world of cybersecurity.

As she drove, she tried not to think too hard about what her father wanted to talk to her about. She had enough weighing on her mind already. She needed to remain clear-headed to deal with Nikki. It had always been like a game of chess between the two of them—only now, the stakes were higher. Back in high school they had vied for status, each trying to eclipse the other in the computer lab. Raven had been more driven by her enjoyment of aggravating Nikki than anything else. The girl couldn't stand to lose, but that also made her dangerous. She didn't understand the concept of cutting your losses and moving on.

It was almost eleven-thirty by the time Raven reached Bridgehaven. She slowed to a crawl as she passed Nikki's mailbox. The split-level house was set far back from the road on a sprawling five-acre lot that backed up to the woods. How on earth was Nikki able to afford a home like that? Raven let out a snort. Apparently, her blackmailing efforts were proving lucrative. Or maybe it wasn't her place. She could be living with someone, a boyfriend, perhaps? Not something that had occurred to Raven before driving out here. But she wasn't overly concerned. With a purple belt in jiu-jitsu, she was confident in her ability to take someone down if she had to.

She drove farther down the street and parked along the curb beneath a leafy oak tree. After switching off the engine, she sent her dad a quick text with Nikki's address. *Just in case you don't hear from me again! Lol!* She had no intention of being the second Golding woman to disappear, but making provision for backup security was part of her trade.

After stuffing her phone into her coat pocket, she walked the short distance back down the street to Nikki's driveway. A tabby cat meowed, watching her from atop a post, eyes glowing yellow orange in the dark. Its matted fur made its scrawny body look like it had more padding than it did. Raven stopped to rub its head. She checked for a collar but found none. "Sorry little fella, I don't have anything to give you."

If the cat was still there when she came back, she would take it home with her. It didn't look like anyone owned it and, if they did, they didn't deserve to. Her mom would make sure it found a good home.

Raven kept her eyes peeled for any signs of movement

around the house as she walked up the steep driveway toward the unassuming single-story home. A red Honda Civic was the only car parked outside, but there could be other vehicles in the garage, and any number of people inside the house. The curtains were pulled in the front room, but she could see the flicker of a TV screen. After assessing the situation, she decided against snooping around outside. If there were other people living here, she didn't want to surprise them into calling the police on her. Tonight's assignment was less about sleuthing and more about subterfuge. Taking a deep breath, she stepped up to the front door and rang the bell. Rubbing her arms, she shivered in the cold, night air.

After a minute or two, she heard footsteps.

"Hello, Nikki," she said, as the door swung inward.

Her eyes widened, but she quickly masked her surprise. "What are you doing here?"

Raven flashed her a sickly-sweet smile. "I'm here to settle my debts."

Nikki arched a skeptical brow. "In that case, you'd better come in."

"Nice digs," Raven said, following her into the kitchen.

"Not that impressive compared to your luxury pad."

Raven swept a gaze around the outdated kitchen, eying a partially open door to a flight of stairs, presumably leading down to a basement. "Are you renting?"

Nikki grinned at her. "I might be buying if you're here to settle your debts."

"Better give me the tour then, so I know where my money's going."

"That's extra."

Raven held her gaze. This was beginning to feel like old

times. *Knight to f3, bishop to e5, checkmate.* “Did my mother come by to see you this evening?”

Nikki threw her a baffled look. ”Why would she come here?”

Raven shrugged. “She said she had to drop something off at an employee’s house. She might have meant Gloria. I wasn’t paying attention.”

“Want a beer?” Nikki asked, opening the refrigerator door.

“No thanks,” Raven replied, eying the contents. One whole shelf was devoted to beer cans and little else. Surely that wasn’t all for Nikki.

“Do you live alone?”

A peculiar smile tugged at Nikki’s lips. ”I have a roommate. Why? Are they kicking you out of Casa Grande?”

Raven gave a hollow laugh. “Not for another few months.”

Nikki pulled the tab on her beer and took a long sip. “You didn’t come all the way here to rent a room. Let’s hear your debt settlement proposal.”

“I can get you $250,000 in a lump sum. But I need your help. It involves a heist of sorts.”

~

Chater 32
Andrew

Andrew woke with a start. He rubbed his hands over his face and sat up on the couch where he’d fallen asleep last night waiting on Raven to return. Glancing at his watch, he was shocked to see that it was almost nine a.m. already. A thread of disquiet pulled at his gut. He went over to the window and peered out through the curtains. Raven's car wasn't parked outside. He checked her old room, but the bed was undisturbed. Had she slept on a friend's couch? Increasingly on edge, he made his way to the kitchen and unplugged his phone from the charger. A message from Raven lit up the screen.

1121 Oak Drive, Bridgehaven. Just in case you don't hear from me again! Lol!

A jolt of fear went through him. He tried calling her number but she didn't pick up. He followed up with several panicked texts. *Are you okay? Where are you? Call me ASAP!* Rubbing a hand over his jaw, he tried to rationalize her absence. She might have stayed over at a friend's place. Maybe she and Sage had worked things out with Nikki and decided to spend the night there. After all, Bridgehaven was an hour's drive away. Or maybe they had stayed at a hotel.

The other side of his brain was bleating out an entirely different kind of distress message. Something might have happened to his daughter. If she was able, surely she would have responded to him by now. Unless she was enjoying making him suffer. He paced back-and-forth trying to decide what to do. If she didn't get back to him by ten, he would drive to the address to see if she was still there—if she'd even made it there in the first place. He wasn't ready to start calling around all the hospitals, but it would be his next step.

He sipped on a black coffee as he scrambled some eggs. Judging by the clamoring hunger pangs, he'd fallen asleep on an empty stomach. After chowing down on the welcome food, he hit the shower. He was toweling off when his phone rang. He frowned at the screen. *Gloria Webber.* Why was Sage's manager calling him?

"Andrew, is Sage there?" she blurted out the minute he picked up.

"No, sorry."

"It's just that she wanted to get an early start this morning on our monthly inventory. I've been waiting here since eight but there's still no sign of her. She's not answering her phone either."

Andrew ran a hand through his damp hair. "To be honest, I have no idea where she is."

"Perhaps you could try calling her?"

He gave an awkward cough. "I don't know if she told you, but we're separated—in the process, at least."

"Oh ... yes. Raven did mention it. Well, I—" Gloria broke off, sounding flustered. "I didn't mean to pry. I'll just get started on the inventory myself."

"Wait! Before you hang up, I don't suppose you've seen Raven, have you?"

"She came by the store yesterday to pick something up."

"What time did she leave?"

"I couldn't tell you exactly. After me. It was ... rather late." After a lengthy pause, she asked. "Is everything all right?"

"Yes, fine," Andrew said dismissively. "I was just hoping Raven would come by last night. She might have bunked at a friend's place. You know how she's been lately."

"Yes," Gloria said, sounding unconvinced. "Please let me know as soon as you hear from Sage. I'm concerned."

Andrew hung up, immediately regretting having asked about Raven. Gloria probably knew all about his affair with the missing girl, and now, to all appearances, his wife and daughter had vanished too. He only hoped Gloria didn't start spreading rumors that might tighten the noose around his neck.

He had just finished getting dressed when his phone rang again with another unwelcome call, this time from the dean.

He forced a smile onto his face, hoping it would infiltrate his tone. "Good morning, John."

"Andrew, the board has discussed your situation, and they feel it would be best if you took a leave of absence. It doesn't look good to have you on campus while the police are still searching for Jemma Knight."

Andrew let out a defeated snort. "You're going to fire me, aren't you? This is just a long-winded path to the end."

The dean cleared his throat. "There's always room to reevaluate, depending on how things unfold."

Andrew grimaced. He would be out of a job if they found a body, even if he was proved innocent. If Jemma had committed suicide, he might as well have killed her in the eyes of the media and community at large. And if she was found alive, they would likely still fire him. They could choose to reprimand him, but the fact that the story had garnered so much attention in the press would work against him. The sooner he accepted his fate, the better for everyone.

After ending the call, he picked up his car keys and went out to the garage. It was time to go look for his daughter and wife. As the door rolled open, he noticed a squad car pulling up to the curb. His heart sank. What now? Was he under arrest again? Had Raven been in an accident? Was Sage having him evicted? He waited in the bowels of his garage, watching as a short, thick-set man exited the car and strode up the driveway. *Meehan!*

The balding officer gave him a dutiful nod. "I'm here to do a welfare check. We have a report of a woman missing from this residence."

32

ANDREW

Andrew gripped his key fob tightly in his fist. How did Meehan know Sage was missing? Or was he here about Raven? Had Gloria called the police to air her suspicions? "Who are you talking about?"

"Sage Golding, your wife." Meehan's hairy brows hugged together.

Andrew gestured resignedly to the door leading into the kitchen. This didn't look good on the heels of Jemma's disappearance. How was he going to explain his wife's absence? "You'd better come in."

Meehan cast a scrutinizing gaze around the space, nostrils flared like a human hound on the prowl for blood, no doubt sniffing the air for any hint of bleach. Andrew tugged nervously at his ear. He was under the microscope again. The number one person of interest in another missing woman's case. Could his life plummet any farther?

Meehan glanced at the notebook he had pulled from his pocket. "We had a call from the manager at Thrifty Tails, a Gloria Webber. She said her employer didn't show up for work this morning, and that you were evasive when she called to ask about her whereabouts." He coughed discreetly. "She's concerned something might have happened to your wife, given the fact that your girlfriend also went missing recently."

Meehan fastened a steely gaze on Andrew, awaiting his response.

He rubbed his damp palms over his thighs. It had been a mistake to involve Gloria. He'd regretted telling her Sage wasn't home the minute he'd hung up with her. Understandably, her allegiance was with her employer. Gloria was leery of him now that she knew their marriage was falling apart. He needed to dig himself out of this pit, and quickly. "I'm worried, too."

Meehan scratched the back of his head. "But you didn't report her missing?"

Andrew averted his gaze. He didn't dare bring up the fact that Raven had gone AWOL as well. He was ninety-nine percent sure he would be marched out of here in handcuffs if he mentioned it. "My wife and I are in the process of separating. We don't keep track of each other's comings and goings."

Meehan eyed him skeptically. "When did you last see your wife?"

"Yesterday."

The detective jotted something down in his notebook. "What was her frame of mind?"

Andrew shrugged. "As you can imagine, we're not exactly engaging in a lot of conversation with one another. She made it clear she wants me to move out—the sooner the better."

Meehan drummed his fingers on the table. "Your girlfriend went missing after you broke up with her, your wife disappears after she asks you to move out, who's next?"

A cold tingle went down Andrew's spine. Did he know about Raven too? Was Meehan toying with him—waiting on him to slip up?

"I'm sure there's a perfectly reasonable explanation for my wife's absence," he answered. "She's a busy woman, on the board of several charitable organizations. She probably had an appointment she forgot to tell Gloria about."

"I hope you're not trying to buy time, Mr. Golding. It won't help you in the end." Meehan placed his card on the table in front of him and tapped on it. "Call me the minute you hear from her. If she doesn't show up by tomorrow, I'll be launching a full investigation." He got to his feet and adjusted his belt. "In the meantime, we'll be monitoring the situation."

After seeing him out, Andrew sank back down at the kitchen table endeavoring to process exactly how much trouble he was in. What did *monitoring the situation* even mean? Were they going to be surveilling him? Was his arrest imminent? He scrubbed his hands over his face, trying to reason with his terrifying thoughts. Sage hadn't been missing long enough to raise any serious red flags, and she wasn't considered a vulnerable person—just another unhappily married woman, as far as the cops were concerned. It was too soon to initiate an official inquiry. But they didn't know the half of it.

He clenched his fists. He had to find out where his daughter was. If he found Raven, it would lead him to Sage. If something nefarious had happened to his family, it was up to him to find them. But he needed a plan. And he couldn't do it alone. He fished his phone from his pocket and dialed the only number he knew he could count on. "Carmen, I'm in trouble."

She gave a corroborating grunt. "Yes, you most certainly are, Professor Golding."

"I need your help again."

She sighed. "I'm not going to go to bat for you with the dean, if that's what you're proposing. The board has already made their decision. I may be of significant proportions but I'm not all that significant when it comes to swaying the consensus around here."

"It's not my job I'm worried about. It's Sage. Her manager at Thrifty Tails reported her missing—she didn't show up for work this morning. The police were just here asking questions."

"Are you serious?" Carmen's voice shot straight into the hysterical range. "You're really scaring me now."

"Calm down. Sage isn't officially missing, yet. I think she might have gone to her new assistant, Nikki's, house last night to talk to her. It was late when she drove out there so it's possible she spent the night at a hotel. But I can't get a hold of her."

Carmen blew out a breath. "Well, that sounds relatively harmless. Maybe she didn't want to stay in the house with you. Aren't you supposed to be moving out? That's probably why she didn't come home."

"The thing is, someone's been blackmailing her., and she thought it might have been Nikki. That's why she went to talk to her."

"Hmm ... so you think they might have got into it or something?"

"That's what I'm afraid of. Raven drove out to Nikki's house last night to look for her mother and she hasn't come back yet either."

33

SAGE

She hadn't expected to die like this. A week ago, she would have thought her chances of succumbing to ALS were considerably higher than taking a bullet to the brain. In the span of a few suspended seconds, the odds had changed.

Jared slid into the passenger seat next to her and pressed the gun into her side. "Drive!"

"I ... I don't understand. Why are you doing this?"

She flinched when he rammed the gun harder into her belly.

"Just shut up and drive!"

She put the car in gear and glanced in her rearview mirror, hoping another car would come by. But the country road was deserted. The dark sedan Jared had abandoned was partially blocking it. No doubt, it was stolen and couldn't be traced back to him. Hopefully, no one would come flying around the corner and crash into it.

"Take a left up here." Jared gestured with the gun to the intersection up ahead.

She bit her lip, trying to remain calm and think clearly.

She was used to taking orders from him, but that had been a long time ago when she was young and senseless. They were both adults now. Not that it helped her current situation. She was at his mercy, once more, and, as Marina had predicted, he had only become more dangerous after being caged up for three decades. Her chest hurt as she pulled a shaky breath, partly from the fist of terror gripping her lungs, partly from the disease chewing at her. She couldn't think about that now. There was only enough adrenaline in her veins for one fight at a time.

She set her mind to figuring out a solution to her immediate dilemma. There wasn't anything she could do to gain the advantage in the moment. Not with both hands on the steering wheel and a gun jammed in her side. Her best bet was to wait until they arrived at their destination and try to make a move then. She still had the syringe filled with tranquilizer medication in her purse, if she could find an opportunity to use it. Until then, she needed to use the time to try and get inside his head.

"Jared, I know you're frustrated and angry, but we can work together to find out who framed you, and who's blackmailing me."

"I'm not interested in a working relationship, and I don't buy your little blackmail cover story."

"It's not a story. I can show you the email demands. Do you really think I would have sought you out for no reason?"

Jared snorted. "You had your reasons. You didn't come here to ask for my help. You thought it was me blackmailing you, didn't you?"

"No! Why would you say that? We trusted each other once."

"Yeah, a long time ago. But, as you reminded me, you

moved on with your precious professor. Turn down this lane up ahead."

Sage grimaced as she made a right turn down a dark, gravel road. She would do anything to be home with her *precious professor* right now. She shivered as she pictured herself lying in a shallow, unmarked grave. It wouldn't be the first time Jared had buried someone who'd betrayed him. "Where are you taking me?"

"Some place quiet to conduct business. You'll find out soon enough."

She swallowed the knot of fear in her throat. She should have known he wouldn't make a move in his mother's house —he needed to be discreet to get the truth out of her. He was taking her somewhere no one would hear her screams.

They drove for half a mile or so before he directed her to turn up an unmarked lane. She could just about make out the outline of a derelict house up ahead. The roof was caved in on one end where a tree had landed on it. It looked like it had been abandoned for at least as long as Jared had been in prison.

"Drive around the back," he ordered her.

Panic fluttered in her throat. They were completely isolated at this location. No neighbors in sight, no lights visible from houses in the distance, only a plump moon monitoring their activity. The perfect location for drugs to exchange hands. And to bury bodies. It appeared Jared was back in business.

She pulled around the back of the house and rolled to a stop outside a tumbledown barn of sorts.

"Not here," Jared said. "Park out of sight behind the barn."

She put the car back into gear and complied.

"Now, get out," he said, waving the gun at her.

She reached for her purse on the console between them. Jared grabbed it from her. "Where's your phone?"

"In my coat."

He pointed the gun at her face. "Pull it out, slowly."

Gingerly, she dug out her phone and held it up. He snatched it out of her hand, then tossed her back her purse. "Let's go."

She threw the strap over her head, and climbed out, legs quivering beneath her.

Jared grabbed her by the arm and shoved her forward. To her dismay, he marched her straight into the shadowy barn. She wrinkled her nose at the smell of decay and disuse. Moonlight spilled through the rotting rafters. Jared rammed her up against a horse stall and zip tied her hands to the grill bars. "Don't try anything stupid," he growled, before retreating out the door.

"Wait! Where are you going?" she screamed after him. " Don't leave me here!"

She wriggled her hands in every direction, but it was impossible to free herself. The zip ties cut into her flesh like blades every time she moved. Her purse was still slung over her shoulder, but it was no use to her with her hands tied to the railing. Why had she ever decided to confront Jared? *Stupid*! She had thought she would be safe as long as his mother was there, but she should have known he wouldn't let her walk away from him that easily a second time.

It was a good fifteen minutes before he returned carrying two rickety wooden spindle chairs and a bottle of whiskey. He cut her free, then secured her to the chair with a rope around her waist before zip tying her hands in front of her. "That's better," he said, giving her a patronizing pat on the cheek. He sank down in the chair opposite, resting the gun on his leg and leered at her. "Comfortable?"

"Why are you doing this?" she fumed.

He raised the bottle to his lips and guzzled down a few mouthfuls. "Do you have any idea what it was like for me stuck behind bars for thirty years for a crime I didn't commit?

Sage painted on a melancholic expression. "I'm sorry, Jared. It must have been awful."

He glanced down at the gun before looking back up at her. "The only thing worse than being abandoned by my woman, was being betrayed by her."

34

RAVEN

Nikki threw Raven a slit-eyed look. "What kind of heist are we talking about? I don't like to get my hands dirty."

She pasted on a disarming grin. "Strictly electronic. No trails leading back to either of us. A clean job. I've picked up a few new tricks along the way."

Nikki sipped her beer, her expression blank. "And who are you intending to steal this money from?"

"Sage and Andrew Golding."

Nikki threw back her head and let out a bark of laughter. "I don't believe you. Why would you rip off your own parents?"

Raven scowled. "I hate them. They're cheats, liars, and hypocrites."

An amused smile danced on Nikki's lips. "I heard about your dad and his little bit on the side. The professor is a player, by all accounts."

"I'll never forgive him for what he did," Raven said, her voice so tight she could almost feel the electricity snapping off it. She wasn't acting anymore. It wasn't hard to drum up the outrage she'd been bottling up inside.

Nikki set her can down on the table and licked her lips. "And your mother? What's your beef with her? Saving kittens and rehousing spiders is hardly grounds for excommunication."

"There's a lot you don't know about her. My do-gooder, holier-than-thou mother was a full-on druggie in her past life. Her ex-boyfriend went to prison for a drug-related murder."

Raven monitored Nikki's reaction closely. She arched a brow, conveying surprise, but she didn't seem overly shocked. If she was the blackmailer, this was information she already had. But it was impossible to read her. She was a sociopath when it came to controlling her emotions—at least the ones she had.

Nikki tapped a fingernail methodically against her beer can. "Let me get this straight. I'm supposed to believe that you hate your parents more than you hate me. You're willing to steal your inheritance and give it to me just to get back at them for being hypocrites."

Raven gave a derisive laugh. "I don't need my parents' lame pension fund. I stand to make more money in my new job in one year than their entire nest egg."

Nikki cocked her head. "So, how exactly is this *heist* going to work?"

"Get your laptop and I'll run through it with you."

Nikki eyed her mistrustfully. "Fine. But if I don't like your plan, you're still on the hook to compensate me. Like I said, I'm not going to get my hands dirty."

"Trust me, it's clean, but it's a two-person job."

Nikki got to her feet and disappeared down the hallway.

The minute she was out of sight, Raven jumped up and walked over to the door leading down to the basement. Sucking in a quick breath, she peered down into the darkness, then took a hesitant step down the stairs. "Hello? Is anyone there?"

She listened for a moment, but there was no response, no sounds of rustling, or anyone moving about. Sensing a presence behind her, she swung around to see Nikki hovering over her. She flashed her an awkward grin. "You said the tour was extra, so I thought I'd take a peek for free."

Nikki shrugged. "If we're going to be working together, I'll throw in the tour." She gestured to the stairs. "After you."

Raven hesitated, her heart beginning to race. It was never a good idea to walk down a flight of stairs in front of your enemy, but if she didn't comply, she might blow her cover. She had to get Nikki to trust her. She needed access to her computer to find out if she was blackmailing her mother.

"Thanks!" She grinned and hurried down the stairs two at a time, just out of arm's reach of Nikki. "Wow! A fully finished basement—nice!"

"Best space in the house," Nikki replied. "I have a workout area with a full-length mirror on the wall over here. And a den, a big screen TV, and a bar—tons of storage space and shelving too."

"What's that room over there, more storage?" Raven asked, gesturing to the closed door at the far end of the basement.

"It's a bedroom with an en suite bathroom. I'd show you but it's my roommate's. She keeps it locked." Nikki walked over to the door and wiggled the knob to prove her point. "She's gone a lot. Kind of an oddball. Not great company, but it helps offset the rent."

Raven bit her lip. It sounded feasible. What was the alternative? Did she really believe Nikki had her mother locked up in there? It was too ridiculous to even consider. She was beginning to think her mother hadn't come here, after all.

But it begged the question: *where was she?*

35

SAGE

Jared took a swig of whiskey from the bottle, his eyes never leaving hers. Sage breathed slowly in and out, weighing her options. Unless she denied everything, she was as good as dead. But she had to toss him some kind of a bone to gnaw on. If she threw Marina under the bus as the snitch who had sold him out, she might be able to alert the police before he struck. But that was assuming he would let her go once she gave him the information he wanted. One thing was for sure—there was nothing to be gained by confessing to the truth of what she'd done all those years ago. He would execute her immediately—he might kill her anyway.

She eyed the bottle he was drinking from with an air of trepidation. The drunker he got, the more dangerous her situation would become. She desperately needed to get her hands on that syringe in her purse. She'd struggled in vain to retrieve it while he'd been fetching the chairs from the house, but the zip ties were cinched too tight on her wrists. She had to get him to trust her enough to remove them.

"I didn't rat you out, Jared, but I have a theory about who

did," she said. "How about you look for a couple of glasses in the house and we can talk about it over a shot of whiskey."

He laughed and ran the back of his hand under his nose. "You don't look like you guzzle whiskey like you used to."

"Doesn't mean I can't have a drink with an old friend."

He gave her the once over, a lecherous glint in his eye. He set the bottle on the floor and got to his feet. "All right. Maybe a shot of whiskey will loosen your lips."

She exhaled in relief when he trudged out of the barn, looking a little unsteady on his feet. Hopefully, he would cut her hands free once he poured her a drink. At least then she'd have a fighting chance. She wished she knew what he'd done with her phone. Not that anyone would be looking for her now that she'd stupidly turned off location sharing with Andrew. A petulant act, but it had felt good at the time to lash out in even the most feeble of ways. Asking him to move out should have felt even better but, in reality, it had torn her up inside. Everything was crashing down around her. She had always prided herself on being strong and resilient, but ALS was draining her, mentally and physically. For once, she wanted to be taken care of, but she'd chased everyone away, including her daughter.

She darted a glance around the barn, taking note of anything and everything that might be of use if she could only get her hands on it. The cavalry wasn't coming to save her. If she was going to get out of this mess, it would be down to her own stubborn will to live. She grimaced at the irony of it. Her stubbornness was what had gotten her into this situation in the first place. She had been way off base thinking Jared had anything at all to do with the blackmail demands. If only she'd listened to Raven and confronted Nikki. How had it got to the point where she didn't trust her own daughter to tell her the truth? It made sense that her newly hired assistant was the one behind the blackmail. She had lied on her job application, she was a proficient hacker, and she had a score to settle with Raven.

Her head jerked in the direction of the door when she heard Jared returning. He held two chipped mugs aloft. " Best I could find in the china cabinet."

Sage painted on an approving grin, inwardly cringing at the thought of the dust and spiderwebs the mugs contained.

Jared walked back to his chair and poured them each a generous shot.

She held out her zip-tied hands with a sheepish look on her face. "It's not as if I'm going anywhere tied to this chair, with you sitting opposite me with a loaded gun."

He let out a scoffing laugh and took a swig from his mug as he considered her plea. "An audacious request. I like the new you." In one swift move, he tugged a knife from his boot and cut the zip ties lashing her hands together. A tremor went through her as he replaced the blade in his boot. He could just as easily have slashed her wrists and left her to bleed out. She was painfully aware of the thin line between life and death she was walking. Experience had taught her that Jared's rage could be triggered in half a heartbeat. She made a show of rubbing her wrists before reaching for the mug he held out to her.

Quashing her fear, she curled her fingers around it and smiled her thanks. For all she knew, he might have put something in her drink. She couldn't risk swallowing it. Keeping a clear head was the most important thing she could do to get out of here in one piece. She took a small sip, wetting her lips and letting the liquid slide back into the mug. A barrage of bad memories came flooding back at the smoky taste on her tongue. She'd been clean and sober for twenty-five years and she had no desire to revert to the drinking habits of her youth that had almost signed her death warrant. Then again, if her diagnosis was terminal, did abstinence even matter anymore? She shook her head to rid herself of her morbid thoughts. *Keep on fighting.*

Jared threw her an amused look. "Too bitter?"

She shrugged. "It's not the worst we've had."

He grunted his agreement. "Whole lot better than the hooch I've been drinking in the pen."

Sage studied him over the rim of her mug. "What was it like—being locked up?"

He took another swig from his mug, a contemplative look on his face. "General population is a gig you get used to. Got its own set of rules, no-go zones, tribes—just like everywhere else on the planet. Everyone lives for the day they get out. Some of them you know are coming right back. Parole hearings come and go, you get your hopes up, you lose hope." He leaned back in his chair and sniffed. "The worst is solitary. I did twenty-five days one time for punching a guy."

"And now you're finally out."

Jared slurped his whiskey and nodded thoughtfully. "Thirty years of my life gone—stolen from me. I've had a long time to plan my retribution."

36

RAVEN

"We'd better get to work," Raven said, turning back toward the stairs. Suddenly, something crashed against the side of her head, the pain reverberating through her body like a diminished chord slammed on a piano. A wave of nausea followed, then spinning stars, then nothing.

When she woke, she was lying in near darkness. A rectangle of moonlight framed by a tiny transom window leant the room she was in only the sparsest of light. She couldn't remember where she was or how she got there. Blinking, she fought to clear the fog from her brain. Why did her head feel so fuzzy? Had she been drinking? She tried to sit up, then groaned, instantly falling back down. Pain radiated out from the side of her head, stabbing her left eye like a sharpened spear. Had she slipped on the marble floors at the Baumgartners? How long had she been lying here? It couldn't have been too long, or the housekeeping staff would have found her by now.

She took a shallow breath and attempted, once more, to sit up. The pain was worse the second time, ripping through her head like wildfire. Terror gripped her. Something was seriously wrong. She must have taken a hard fall and knocked herself out—was she concussed? Cautiously, she raised her hand to her head and felt around to assess the damage. A blood-encrusted lump the size of a golf ball protruded out the side of her head.

She patted the floor around her, but it wasn't the cold, smooth feel of marble she'd expected to find. She was lying on some kind of mat—not the high-end luxury mattress she enjoyed at the Baumgartners' residence. Where was she?

She dampened her dried-out lips. "Hello?" she called out weakly. "Is anyone there?" Breath on pause, she waited, clinging to the hope that someone had heard her pitiful attempt to call for help. Minutes went by, but no one came to her aid.

Despite the stabbing pain in her head, her eyes were beginning to adjust to her shadowy surroundings. Her confused gaze zigzagged across the space like a grasshopper. She was in a small, sparsely furnished room. She furrowed her brow, trying again to remember how she'd got here. Her head throbbed harder, and then it came back to her with a jolt. *Nikki's house*! She'd been showing her around the basement. What on earth had happened? Had she tripped on the stairs? That would explain why her head was exploding with pain. Images of the space flashed to mind. The workout area, the den, the built-in bar, the storage shelves. *The roommate's bedroom!* Was that where she was? Had Nikki offered to let her spend the night?

She scrunched her eyes shut, then froze at the sound of a moan coming from the other side of the room. Turning her head slowly, she peered into the darkness. She could just about make out a figure curled up on a sleeping mat. Her eyes widened. Was the roommate here, after all? Why hadn't

Nikki said anything? Maybe she'd arrived back late at night after Raven was already ensconced in her room. Her heart thudded faster. None of this made any sense.

Cautiously, she patted the side of her head again, wincing when she felt the massive lump that was causing her so much pain. She couldn't remember falling. She had turned toward the stairs and then—BAM! The breath left her lungs as it came back to her. The blow had come from behind. Someone must have cracked her on the head. Was it the elusive roommate? Nikki had said she was an oddball—did that mean she was dangerous? Gingerly, she twisted her head and peered through the darkness once more. "Nikki, is that you?" She held her breath but got no response. Somehow, she had to make the effort to crawl over there and see who was in the room with her. Nikki was unstable, but it was possible her mysterious roommate who came and went at will, and kept herself to herself, was even more deranged. Maybe she'd attacked them both in a fit of jealous rage.

Raven let out a gasp when she suddenly remembered the reason she'd come here in the first place. *Her mother!* Nikki had acted as though she hadn't seen her, but she could have been lying. Had she attacked her, and her mother too? Was that who was moaning on the other side of the room? Adrenaline coursed through her at the thought of her mom lying mere feet away. She might be injured, bleeding—dying. She had to get to her, make sure she was okay.

Groaning, Raven rolled cautiously first onto her side, then onto her stomach. She rested face down on her hands for several minutes, breathing through the pain. If there was one thing jiu-jitsu had taught her, it was mental fortitude. She wasn't sure she could stand, let alone walk—she was far too dizzy. Army crawling across the floor would test her threshold for pain like never before, but she'd trained her mind for moments like this.

She forced herself to focus as she pushed up on her forearms and drew her left foot to her side. Inching forward, she repeated the process, dragging her right leg into position. This might prove to be her biggest test of endurance to date. Gritting her teeth against the pain, she continued onward, forcing her reluctant limbs into submission, eyes firmly focused on the shadowy figure on the other side of the room. With every tiny movement, it felt as though someone was drumming heavy metal inside her head, but she resolvedly tuned it out, empowered by the hours she'd spent in the gym, pushing through every barrier.

When she finally reached the mat on the other side of the room, she reached out and tugged the thin blanket off the figure curled beneath it.

37

RAVEN

Raven stared in disbelief at the battered young woman sleeping on the mat in front of her, dirty blonde hair fanned out around her. She was dressed in an oversized T-shirt and sweats, her small frame lost in the baggy ensemble. Raven's head pounded, her splintered thoughts grappling to form a coherent picture. The woman's face was vaguely familiar. Where had she seen her before? In one of her college classes? The name came to her like a jolt of electricity zapping her aching brain. *Jemma Knight. The missing girl!* Alive, but barely, if her appearance was anything to go by. Was she injured, or drugged—both? Raven did a cursory examination, squinting in the darkness, but could find no apparent wounds.

She sank back down on the floor, exhausted by the effort of dragging herself across the room in a concussed state. What was Jemma Knight doing here? Was this where she'd been hiding from the police? Was she the roommate Nikki had been referring to, or was she being held here against her will? Raven blinked over at the door, her fingers curling into fists. Maybe they both were. She had to find out.

Slowly, she maneuvered herself around to face the door and began the slow crawl toward it. The pain ratcheted up a notch, but she focused on her destination, visualizing each small movement before executing it. When she finally reached the door, she took a few minutes to get her wind back before attempting to pull herself to her feet. The room spun around her, and she leaned her forehead against the cool wall until things began to stabilize. Tentatively, she stretched out a hand and twisted the doorknob. *Locked*! She jiggled it several times for good measure, before giving up and sliding down the wall into a sitting position.

Now what? She was in too much pain to try kicking the door down, and Jemma was in no state to help her. She patted her pockets, confirming her suspicion that her phone was gone, which left her with no way to contact anyone for help. Banging on the door would be a waste of energy. Nikki would return when Nikki wanted to return. All she could do was wait until she made an appearance and try to reason with her. She scrunched her eyes shut. That would be no easy feat. It was clear Nikki was willing to do whatever it took to destroy her—even going so far as to frame her family for murder.

Groaning, Raven began the painfully slow process of returning to her mat. This time, she forced herself to walk the entire way, trudging unsteadily along the wall with zombie-like steps. Her gaze landed on a bucket in the opposite corner of the room. A roll of toilet paper sat on the floor next to it. She wrinkled her nose. So much for the en suite bathroom. Sinking back down on her makeshift bed with a tired sigh, she closed her eyes and gingerly rested the uninjured side of her head on the thin mat. The fog inside her brain was gradually beginning to clear. She wasn't in any physical state to do much about her circumstances, but her mental faculties were still there. She had to come up with a plan before Nikki returned.

She could offer her money, but she had a feeling that wasn't what Nikki was really after. She'd already tried that and look what had happened. It was increasingly clear that the kind of compensation Nikki wanted was vengeful, not financial. If she wasn't going to listen to reason, or accept a bribe, then the only way Raven was getting out of here was to overpower her. It shouldn't have been a problem, given her fitness level and training. But she was at a severe disadvantage after taking the blow to the head.

The other variable in the equation was whether Nikki was armed. It was reasonable to assume she was. And she might not be working alone either. The fridge was well-stocked with beer, suggesting a male companion. The best thing Raven could do for now was to get some rest and try to heal. Maybe by the time the sun rose, she would be in better shape to defend herself.

She woke to a strange tickling sensation. And a hand pressed firmly over her mouth.

38

ANDREW

Andrew pulled up outside Carmen's house and left the engine idling as he plugged Nikki's address into his GPS. He peered anxiously out through the window until he saw the lights go out in the house and Carmen emerge in the doorway carrying a plastic bag. As she shuffled over to the car, he jumped out and opened the passenger door for her. "I can't thank you enough for helping me out."

She gave him her infamous eye roll as she hefted her weight into the seat. "Just so we're clear, I'm only the look-out. I don't sprint, I don't tackle, and I brought snacks."

He laughed as he put the car into gear. He missed all the daily sparring and witty exchanges he enjoyed with his colleagues. He couldn't help wondering how long it would take the board to formally ask him to step down. He'd resigned himself to the fact that they would bring the hammer down on him—it was only a matter of when. "What are they saying about me at work?" he ventured, bracing himself for Carmen's answer.

She grunted. "Not pleasant things. Nothing worth repeating."

"I figured as much. What's the general consensus—do they think I had something to do with Jemma's disappearance?"

"We're *way* beyond that, my friend." Carmen reached into the bag she had brought and pulled out a half-eaten package of chips. "Speculation about what a professor of medieval literature is capable of in his free time defies the imagination. Everything from chopping up your student and hiding her body parts, to forcing her into a cult."

Andrew swallowed back the bile surging up his throat. It was heartless, sickening gossip, but he deserved as much. He had brought this on himself.

"Here," Carmen said, thrusting the bag his way. "Sucking on salt is better than licking your wounds."

"Thanks." Andrew grabbed a handful of chips and placed them in his lap. He wasn't much of a snacker, but he could use something to distract himself during the drive.

"So, tell me about this Nikki Patterson," Carmen said.

"I know very little—only what Raven has relayed to me. They had some kind of rivalry going on back in high school. Raven won a major scholarship that Nikki was a shoe-in for, and she's held a grudge against her ever since. That's the gist of it. I don't know how much of it is true. I hate to say my own daughter could be lying to me, but it feels as though something's missing from the story."

Carmen crunched through a mouthful of chips. "What do you mean?"

"Why would a rival from high school come after her all these years later just because she took a scholarship out from under her?"

Carmen cocked her head to one side. "Maybe Nikki

discovered something that would have changed the outcome."

"What do you mean?"

"Well, it's kind of like when you find new evidence in a cold case. It suddenly makes the whole thing worth taking a second look."

Andrew frowned, mulling over Carmen's words. She had a point. Had Nikki found out something that prompted her to blackmail Raven? Had his daughter done something illegal? She was certainly more than capable of hacking her way to a sizable scholarship. His heart sank. It appeared Raven and her mother had both been hiding a questionable past from him. Or maybe he'd been too wrapped up in his own world to notice the red flags.

"Is that car following us?" Carmen asked, leaning forward and peering into the side mirror, before turning and looking pointedly over her shoulder.

Andrew glanced in his rearview mirror. They were halfway to Bridgehaven, and the sedan several car lengths behind them had been tailing them most of the way out of the city. It could be a coincidence, but given Meehan's parting shot about *monitoring the situation*, there was a good chance it was an undercover cop tailing him. His pulse began to thud in his throat. Did they really think he had abducted Jemma Knight? The last thing he needed right now was a cop pulling him over. How would he explain why he was driving his car this late at night with another woman on board when his wife and ex-girlfriend had both been reported missing?

And if he told the truth, it would be even harder to explain away the fact that his daughter was also unaccounted for.

39

RAVEN

Raven stared through the chaotic halo of blonde hair dangling over her face into the frenzied blue eyes of the woman preventing her from screaming. Apparently, Jemma Knight hadn't been quite as close to death as Raven had imagined.

"Don't make a sound when I take my hand away," Jemma muttered.

Raven nodded her agreement, gulping in a deep breath when the fingers clamped to her mouth finally lifted. "What are you doing here?" she gasped.

Jemma twisted her lips. "I could ask you the same thing. There's no time for all that now. We have to make a plan before she gets back, or she'll drug us both."

Raven flinched as she pushed herself up on her elbows. She felt considerably better than she did last night, but her head still radiated pain, and she was weak from not eating. "Do you have any water?"

Jemma got up and retrieved a plastic water bottle from her mat. "We'll have to share."

Raven gratefully glugged down several mouthfuls.

"Thanks, I needed that." She wiped the back of her hand over her mouth and cast a curious glance at Jemma, who was pacing around the room eying the sparse contents with a frustrated look on her face. "There's nothing in here we can use as a weapon," she ranted. "We can hardly strangle her with a blanket."

"Do you know who I am?" Raven asked, interrupting her demented gait.

"Seriously? Do we have to do this now?" Jemma huffed.

Raven arched a brow. "Do what?"

"You know—introductions and all."

"I'll take that as a yes. Was my mother here last night?"

Jemma scowled. "Did I look like I was capable of knowing anything that happened last night?"

Raven sighed. "The police are looking for you. They think my father abducted you, possibly killed you."

Jemma sniffed indignantly. "That was the intention."

A chill ran down Raven's spine. "What do you mean? Are you here of your own volition?"

"I was, until I wasn't anymore."

Raven let out an exasperated snort. "We don't have time for games. Why don't you tell me how you ended up here, and then we can make a plan to get out of here."

Jemma stopped pacing and folded her arms in front of her. "Nikki Patterson approached me one day after class. She said she knew about my affair with Andrew, and that he had broken things off. She told me what you did to her, and how much she hated you. She suggested we team up to punish you and your family." Jemma's shoulders slumped. "It was only supposed to be for a day or two, but when I told her I wanted to go home, she flipped out. That's when she forced me at gunpoint to drink some kind of sedative. Next thing I know I'm locked up down here and all my clothes are gone. She comes down once or twice a day and brings me food and water—keeps me drugged up most of the time."

"Can't you fight back?"

Jemma threw her a sour look. "She has a gun. She's crazy. But with two of us, we might have a chance."

Raven's gaze traveled around the room once more, searching for inspiration. "What about the transom window? If we can get it open, one of us could crawl through it."

"How are we supposed to reach it?"

"You're lighter than me. You can try standing on my shoulders." Raven got to her feet, swaying back on her heels for a minute or two.

"Are you all right?" Jemma studied her, frowning. "You're the color of chalk."

"Nikki cracked me on the side of the head. Probably with one of those dumbbells sitting around out there. Try not to kick my skull when you're climbing up on my shoulders."

She walked over to the transom window and squatted in place, interlinking her fingers so Jemma could step up. Squatting was ordinarily an easy position for her to hold, and Jemma looked like she weighed next to nothing. Still, she grimaced when the girl put first one shaky foot and then the other on her shoulders, triggering fresh waves of pain through her head. "You're trying too hard to keep your balance. Just relax and breathe. Can you get it open?"

"It's locked," Jemma replied, wiggling the handle. "I could try breaking the glass, but I don't have anything to smash it with."

Raven gritted her teeth. If she could get up there, she might be able to pull it off. She doubted Jemma had the strength, but it was worth taking a stab at it. "Okay, climb back down and we'll figure something out," She winced when Jemma's foot scraped the side of her head as she dismounted.

"Take your blanket and wrap it around your forearm," Raven instructed her, watching as she twisted it several times. "That'll do. Now, give it another go."

Back in position, Jemma made several labor-intensive attempts to break the window, but to no avail.

"Use your elbow and aim for the corner of the glass," Raven urged.

"Ouch, that hurt," Jemma whined.

"Not as much as my shoulders. Try—"

The words died on her lips at the sound of a key rattling in the door.

40

SAGE

Sage faked a smile, inwardly quivering at Jared's menacing threat. "So, what exactly does your plan of retribution entail when you find this traitor?"

He tapped the barrel of the gun on his knee, studying her with a steely gaze. The menacing flame tattoos creeping up the side of his face flexed as the hard chords in his neck tightened. "That's between me and the snitch. If I told you, I'd have to kill you." He threw back his head and laughed raucously.

Sage did her best to laugh along with him, while masking the terror riding around on a roller coaster in her belly. She could read him like a book. He suspected her, but he had to be certain. It was time to redirect his suspicions. She couldn't in good conscience throw Marina under the bus, even for a temporary stay of execution. It was too risky. But there was another name who wouldn't be hurt by her baseless accusations—someone who deserved to have his reputation trashed. He'd been Jared's righthand man back in the day, and he'd tried to make a move on her after Jared had gone to prison. He hadn't taken it well when she'd rejected his advances.

"I think I know who ratted you out," she said.

Jared took a long draft of whiskey, his eyes never leaving hers over the rim of his mug. "I'm listening."

"Axel Gundersen."

"Axel?" Jared wrinkled his brow. "He got knocked off by the cops a few months after I went to the slammer."

Sage leaned forward in her chair. "I know. The thing is, he kept coming around to see me every time I went to visit you in prison—trying to find out what we talked about, asking if you'd mentioned him at all. He always wanted a blow-by-blow account of what you and I discussed. He was insistent. At first, I didn't think anything of it—he'd taken over the operation from you, after all. But when it kept happening, it made me question what he was really after." She dropped her gaze. "He tried to make a pass at me. It was almost as though he was trying to replace you in every way."

A deep crease formed on Jared's brow. Sage could sense the tension radiating off him as he squeezed his fists—fists she was all too familiar with.

Jared scowled at her. "Why didn't you tell me this at the time?"

She shrugged helplessly. "I was seventeen and scared. He was running the business in your absence. I didn't want to cross him."

Jared got to his feet and began pacing back-and-forth across the floor. He seemed to be considering what she was saying, but even if he believed her, Axel was dead. The only person left to take his revenge out on now was her. She had taken a risk by naming the snitch thirty years later, but it was a better option than confessing to the truth.

"He came to see me in prison one time," Jared said, squaring his jaw. "Couple of months after I got locked up."

A prickling fear blistered over her skin. She raised her brows nonchalantly. "You never told me that. What was that about?"

"He wanted to warn me about someone he was suspicious of. He told me they couldn't be trusted—that they'd set me up to take the fall for Viper Gomez's murder." Jared gave a tight shake of his head. "I didn't believe Axel at the time. He never did come up with any information to prove it, and he was dead a short time later. But, as the years went by, I began to wonder if he'd been on to something."

Sage gave a somber nod, quaking inside. "I was relieved when he stopped coming around. I didn't find out until weeks later that he'd died."

Jared reached for the empty whiskey bottle and got to his feet. "I've got another one of these stashed in the house. We should drink one to his memory." He turned and stared straight at her. "Axel was a good guy. Loyal to the end."

The minute he disappeared through the barn door, Sage let her mug drop to the straw-covered floor. It rolled beneath her chair, resting on its handle. Keeping one eye trained on the door, she fished frantically in her purse for the syringe. She slipped it up her sleeve and wiped the sweat from her brow. Despite the cool temperature in the barn, her body was awash with adrenaline. She couldn't kid herself any longer into thinking Jared believed her. He could see straight through her amateurish attempt to deflect the blame. She might as well have come right out and admitted her guilt. He was setting her up for retribution. Her stomach twisted with fear as she pictured her fate. She doubted he was going to fetch another bottle of whiskey. More like a pitchfork to finish her off with. A bullet to the head would be too civil for him. She tugged at the rope binding her to the chair, but it was knotted behind her back, impossible to loosen.

She shifted nervously in her seat when she heard Jared returning. She needed to keep her wits about her. The next few minutes could be critical. She couldn't afford to hesitate to use the syringe when her chance came. Her life hung in the balance.

Jared held an unopened whiskey bottle aloft. "Madam?"

She gestured to her mug on the floor, holding her breath when he pulled the stopper from the bottle. As he bent down to pick up her mug, she deftly slid the syringe from her sleeve and jabbed it into his upper arm.

He let out a roar and spun around, snarling at her like a wild dog as the whisky bottle flew out of his hand and smashed. She shrank back in her seat. She couldn't tell how much of the tranquilizer medication had gone in, but by all appearances, it had only ramped up his adrenaline. He grabbed her by the throat and began to squeeze. She gasped, eyes bulging, panic overtaking her as the pressure inside her head began to build. The opportunity to reason with him had come and gone in half a heartbeat. She couldn't help wondering if he would break her neck before her head exploded.

His raging red face was the last thing she saw before everything went black.

41

RAVEN

Jemma clambered awkwardly down from Raven's shoulders just as the door swung open and Nikki stepped into the room holding a gun in her hand. "I thought I heard some nocturnal activity down here in the rat pen. Looks like the newest patient has made a swift recovery." She gestured with her gun to the mats. " Back to bed, ladies. I brought you a little something to calm your nerves." She tossed a tumbler to Jemma. "Drink half and give the rest to lover boy's baby girl. I'm glad you two finally had a chance to get acquainted. I'm sure you have lots to talk about."

Jemma looked white as a sheet. All her bravado had vanished at the sight of the gun. Moving in mechanical motions, she slowly unscrewed the lid from the tumbler.

Raven sucked in a hard breath. Nothing would prevail upon her to drink whatever Nikki was using to drug Jemma. She had to keep her wits about her if they had any chance of getting out of here. "I need to see a doctor."

An amused grin danced on Nikki's lips. "Isn't your daddy a doctor? Or is he only a practitioner of medieval alchemy?"

Raven clenched her jaw. All the power was in Nikki's hands, and she was clearly enjoying every minute of it. "Do you have any idea of the kind of charges you're going to be facing—extortion, blackmail, kidnapping, drugging a victim, for starters? You'll never get away with this."

Nikki narrowed her eyes and took a step toward her, holding the gun out in front of her. Raven pulled herself up to her full height, locking a defiant gaze on her nemesis—an all too familiar standoff. Nikki's eyeballs bulged, radiating pure hatred.

Without warning, Jemma hurled the tumbler at Nikki and made a mad dash for the door. Nikki yelled, spun around, and fired. To Raven's horror, Jemma slumped in the doorway, writhing in pain as she clutched her leg.

Adrenaline flooded through Raven's veins, drowning out the pain in her head as her training kicked in. She lunged at Nikki, wrapping both arms around her waist, then dropping her weight suddenly, throwing her to the ground. Nikki's head hit the floor with a sickening crunch. Panting, Raven grabbed the gun and staggered over to the door where Jemma lay sprawled on the floor. "Can you walk?"

"I don't know," Jemma sobbed.

"Okay, listen up. I'm going to pull you to your feet and then lean on me. You can do this. We have to get out of here."

Gritting her teeth, Raven concentrated all her energy on hauling Jemma to her feet. The effort left her reverberating with pain, despite Jemma being a lightweight. The minute they had hobbled their way out of the basement bedroom, Raven slammed the door and turned the key. There was no way Nikki could escape out of this prison of her own making. She took a few shallow breaths. She could see white dots and stars, but she fought to stay upright as she helped Jemma limp over to the den area and settle onto a couch.

Raven cast a despairing glance at the flight of steps leading up to the kitchen. She doubted Jemma would be able to make it up the stairs in her current condition. Even if she could, it would take too long. "I'm going upstairs to find a phone to call for help," Raven said, placing the gun on the couch next to Jemma. "You'll be safe here for a few minutes. She can't get out of the room."

"No! Don't leave me!" Jemma wailed.

"I'll be right back. I have to get help. Here, take this." She pulled off her sweatshirt and pressed it to Jemma's leg before giving her hand a reassuring squeeze. At a quick glance, the wound looked to be superficial, but Jemma was clearly in shock. "Keep pressure on it. I won't be long."

She gritted her teeth as she made her way over to the bottom of the stairs. She wasn't in much better shape than Jemma, but at least her legs still worked. She clung to the railing, hauling herself up one step at a time. Would she be free and clear once she reached the kitchen, or was there someone else in the house? Maybe Nikki's roommate was actually her partner. Or had she been alluding to Jemma in jest? Raven took a deep breath and continued dragging herself up the rest of the way, determined to push through the throbbing pain. If she could locate her phone, she could use that to raise the alarm.

By the time she reached the last step, her heart was thumping so hard she was half-afraid she was on the verge of having a heart attack. The room spun around her, leaving her disoriented. She sank down to the floor until the dizzy spell abated. When she felt able to get going again, she pulled herself to her feet. She swept a gaze over the tile countertops but there was no sign of her phone anywhere.

Slowly, she made her way down the hall, stopping intermittently to lean against the wall. She checked in each of the bedrooms on the off chance there was a phone in one of them, but she couldn't find a landline or a computer anywhere in the house. Her thoughts spiraled downward. She was left with no choice but to leave the house to seek help. Her car was parked further down the road, but she wasn't sure she could drive with a concussion. Her best bet was to walk to the nearest neighbor—if she could make it there without keeling over.

She trudged back up the hall and called down the basement stairs to Jemma. "I can't find a phone. I'm going to the neighbor's to call for help."

"Please don't leave me here alone with her!" Jemma cried.

"She's unconscious and locked in. She can't touch you. I promise I'll be as quick as I can."

Doing her best to tune out Jemma's panicked shrieks, she stumbled down the hall to the front door.

The air outside felt unusually cold without her sweatshirt. She could feel herself losing body heat. She needed to move quickly. As she staggered down toward the road, her only hope was that she wouldn't pass out before she managed to raise the alarm. When she finally reached the bottom of the driveway, she ran out onto the road, at a loss to know which direction to go for help.

All of a sudden, she was almost blinded by headlights. She raised an arm to protect her eyes, fear gripping her as a car barreled toward her.

42

SAGE

When Sage came to, she was slumped forward in a chair. It took her a moment to remember where she was, and what had happened. She swallowed what felt like a blockage in her throat, wincing at the stabbing pain. Her eyes stung and her vision was blurred. Her neck felt like it was aflame—even breathing seemed too harsh an action. She wriggled her body, confirming that she was still tied to the chair. Slowly, the interior of the barn came into focus. Her eyes shot wide open when she spotted a body lying on the floor a few feet in front of her. *Jared*! The tranquilizer had worked! Frantically, she twisted her body again, desperate to break free, but there was no way of loosening the rope around her waist. She was tempted to scream for help, but she was too hoarse—not that anyone would hear her. And what if her efforts to call for help woke Jared? Her window of escape could be short. She had no way of knowing how long the sedative would keep him knocked out.

Her gaze fell on his combat boots. If she could get her hands on his knife, she could cut herself free. But it would require some dangerous maneuvering—rocking her chair until it tipped over and then dragging herself by her hands across the floor. The biggest danger was hitting her head when she fell. But if she didn't do something, she was as good as dead anyway. There was no point in overthinking it. With grim resolve, she began rocking slowly from side to side, concentrating on her freedom at stake, and not the fear frothing in her belly. She let out an involuntary yelp when the chair finally toppled over. Holding out her hands, she managed to avoid slamming her head into the ground. Her left wrist buckled, and, for one terrifying moment, she thought she'd snapped it. Gingerly, she moved it back-and-forth. Sprained but not broken—she could live with that.

Using her hands to maneuver herself into position, she crawled like a turtle over to Jared, the wooden chair tied to her back. She stared at his unmoving body, her resolve faltering. She was half-afraid the minute she reached for the knife his hand would grab hers—like a scene from a horror movie. A stab to the heart would be the final reward for her betrayal. But she had to gamble if she wanted to live.

She shifted awkwardly into position, flinching when she bumped Jared's foot. She froze, but there was no reaction. Fingers moving in slow motion, she grasped the hem of his jeans and raised it a couple of inches revealing the hilt of the knife jutting out from his boot sheath. She curled her fingers around it and slowly withdrew the blade. Trembling, she retreated a few feet on her hands and knees before sawing frantically at her bonds.

After what seemed like an eternity, the rope finally began to fray, then snapped. Sage staggered to her feet, her stiff muscles fighting her every move. Her throat burned. She needed water desperately. But she wanted to live even more. Turning to leave, she spotted Jared's gun a few feet away. It must have skidded out of his hand when he fell unconscious. This was her opportunity to eliminate him, once and for all. But could she bring herself to shoot him? Should she take the chance? She didn't want to go down for murder—Carol would be able to testify that she'd been the last person to see Jared. She chewed on her bottom lip. *Too risky.* But she had to get rid of the gun. In desperation, she kicked it under a pile of rotting tarps nearby, then threw the knife in after it. If he came back around, he would assume she had taken the weapons with her. All she needed to do now was get out of there.

She staggered over to the barn door, her legs adjusting to walking once more. It was almost light outside. Somehow, she had made it through the night. She lurched over to her car and wrenched the door open. Her heart sank when she realized the key fob was missing from the console where she'd left it. Jared must have taken it at some point after he'd tied her up.

Panic set in as she frantically checked the passenger side glove box and rummaged around in the door pockets, to no avail. She buried her face in her hands. He might have the key on him, but there was no way she was going back inside the barn. If he woke, he would finish her off this time. He might already be stirring for all she knew. She couldn't sit here commiserating with herself any longer. She needed to figure out something. There was a chance he'd taken the key fob into the house. She clambered out of the car and stumbled into the musty building, sweeping her gaze around the dilapidated interior. It looked like Jared had been using the space for illegal recreational drug use in direct violation of his parole. Several dirty mattresses lay around the room, and a few discarded needles, pipes, and spoons were scattered over the floor.

She was wasting time here. She needed to get out to the main road and flag down a car. People would be heading out to work soon. Surely someone would stop for a disheveled woman waving desperately at them.

The only question was whether she could make it to the main road before Jared caught up with her.

43

ANDREW

"Should I pull over and let the sedan pass?" Andrew asked, his scalp prickling with sweat.

Carmen cast a probing glance over her shoulder. "No need. He's slowing down. Looks like he's hanging a left at that intersection we just went through."

Andrew's shoulders slackened, relief seeping through him. He'd dodged a bullet—for now. But the police would turn the heat up on him if Sage didn't resurface soon.

With Carmen navigating, they pulled into Bridgehaven a short time later. Her head swiveled like a bird as she talked. "Turn right up ahead at the hospital, then left onto Oak Drive. We're looking for 1121. Hard to read the numbers at night."

"That's Raven's car!" Andrew yelled, pointing to a gray Volkswagen parked under a large oak tree.

"Are you sure?" Carmen asked, squinting into the darkness. "Doesn't look like anyone's in it. She must have gone inside. Keep driving. The house is a little farther down the street."

Andrew slowed to a crawl and slammed the shifter into

park. "I'm just going to take a quick look, make sure she's not asleep in her car." He climbed out and tried the Volkswagen's handle. *Locked*. Tenting his hands over his eyes, he peeked in through the windows before darting back to his own car. "Yeah, she must be in the house," he said to Carmen.

He put the car in gear and drove on down the street, slamming on his brakes when someone came running out into the middle of the road. His eyes widened in disbelief. *Raven*! He swung over to the curb, jumped out and ran to envelop her in a hug, grimacing when he saw the matted, bloody hair on the side of her head. "What happened, honey? Are you okay?" He reached out a hand to touch her head but she grabbed his wrist.

"Don't! It hurts."

"Did Nikki do this to you? We need to take you to the hospital. Is your mom here?"

"No," Raven rasped. "Jemma is."

His jaw dropped, the words hitting him like a punch to the gut. "I ... I don't understand. What's she doing here?"

"Nikki was holding her hostage. It's a long story. She's been shot—I need your help to get her out of there. I managed to lock Nikki in the basement bedroom, but I don't know if anyone else is working with her. She mentioned something about a roommate."

"Where exactly is Jemma?"

"I'll show you."

"No. You stay here with Carmen. Just tell me where she is, and I'll get her."

"She's on the couch in the basement. You access it through a door at the far end of the kitchen. Whatever you do, don't unlock the bedroom door down there. I tackled Nikki, and she knocked herself out when she fell, but if she comes back around, there's no telling what she'll do."

Raven swayed back on her feet, and Andrew reached out a hand to steady her, before helping her into the back seat.

"Lock the doors and keep a close eye on her. She has a head injury," he told Carmen. "Jemma's in the house. She's been shot. I'm going to get her."

He slammed the car door shut, then turned and jogged up the driveway to the house bathed in darkness. His heart knocked against his ribs as he tried to envision what awaited him. Nikki might have escaped for all he knew. Jemma might already be dead. The thought shook him to the core. He pictured the police converging on the house and finding him in the basement with a dead Jemma in his arms. How would he talk his way out of that scenario? He shook his head free of the disturbing thought, forcing his legs to pump harder. By the time he reached the front door, he was heaving for breath. He was badly out of shape—too much time spent pontificating in lecture halls and not enough hours pumping iron at the gym.

The front door lay wide open. Tentatively, he peered inside the shadowy hallway, trying to get his bearings. It was an older house that hadn't been renovated in years, lending it an eerie atmosphere. He made his way slowly down the hallway, peering briefly into the family room as he went by. When he reached the kitchen, he hurried over to the door leading down to the basement. "Jemma, it's Andrew. I'm coming down there to get you," he called out.

She burst out sobbing the minute she heard his voice.

He bolted down the stairs and knelt on the floor next to the couch. "You have no idea how relieved I am to see you! I didn't know if you were dead or alive."

"You came for me!" She smiled at him through teary eyes. "I can't believe you came for me."

He pursed his lips tightly together. He needed to nip this adulation in the bud. He wasn't her knight in shining armor, and he wasn't about to lead her on for a second time. "Not exactly. I came looking for Raven."

Jemma blinked sheepishly at him. "I'm sorry, Andy. It wasn't my idea."

He narrowed his eyes. "What are you talking about?"

"Nikki talked me into disappearing to make the police think you had abducted me. When I said I'd had enough, she drugged me and locked me in the basement bedroom."

Andrew fought to keep his expression even. His hunch had been right all along. It had been a dumb idea with dire consequences, but he was hardly in a position to pass judgement.

"We'll talk about it later. We've got to get out of here, now. Put your arms around my neck."

The minute he swooped her into his arms, she began sobbing again. "It hurts."

"Just breathe through it. Try and hang in there. I'm going to take you straight to the hospital as soon as I get you out of here, but I can't talk and climb the stairs at the same time."

He trudged his way up the staircase, terrified with every step he took that Nikki would break out of the room and lunge up the stairs after them. When he reached the kitchen, he stopped for a minute to catch his breath, then carried Jemma outside. The fresh air invigorated him, and he quickened his pace. The minute he reached the car, Carmen and Raven jumped out to help him.

"Let her sit up front—more leg room," Carmen suggested.

He gingerly set Jemma down on the passenger seat, then

let out a long, relieved breath. "I'll drive the girls to the hospital. It'll be quicker than waiting on an ambulance. Carmen, can you take Raven's car home? I'll pick it up tomorrow."

"No!" Raven cried. "I'm not going to the hospital. Not until I find Mom."

Andrew frowned. "How do you intend to do that at this time of night?"

"I've been thinking about that phone number on the desk in the office. Maybe Carol's a friend of Mom's and she decided to stay there until you move out. Whoever she is, she might know something."

44

ANDREW

"Like it or not, you need to get checked out," Andrew said. "The hospital's only five minutes from here. You'll be no help finding your mom if it turns out you have a serious head injury."

"I don't usually listen to your father either, but he's making sense, for once," Carmen said, holding out her hand for Raven's keys. "I doubt this Carol person, whoever she is, will appreciate being woken up at this time of night anyway."

Raven scowled but, to Andrew's relief, she relented and climbed into the back seat of his Lexus. Carmen stuck her head inside and pointed to the grocery bag at her feet. "I brought snacks. I'm not sure how much they fed you in captivity, but they're all yours."

Raven flashed her a hollow smile. Andrew could tell she wasn't convinced it was a good idea to wait until morning to continue the search for her mother, but she was in no fit state to drive herself home. On the surface, he was trying to appear calm, but he was worried sick about her head injury. A professor in his department had skied into a tree and hit his head this past winter. He'd continued skiing, blissfully unaware that his brain was swelling, and died later that same night.

Andrew climbed in behind the wheel and started up the engine. "Call 911," he said, passing his phone back to Raven. "We need to make sure Nikki's arrested before she has a chance to escape. Let them know we're en route to the hospital."

He listened as Raven relayed the gist of what had gone down to the emergency dispatcher, with Jemma chipping in to confirm her identity.

"They're going to pick Nikki up, and they're sending officers to meet us at the hospital," Raven said when she hung up.

Andrew tried to ignore the dread fermenting in his stomach as he pulled up outside the emergency room doors. No doubt, the police would question the veracity of their story. What if Nikki had already escaped? Even if she was still in the house, there was no guarantee she would confess to anything. And what if Jemma lied and said he'd been the one holding her captive all this time? They could dismiss Raven's testimony as his daughter wanting to protect him. He grimaced as he unplugged his seatbelt. He knew he was being paranoid, but it was hard to think logically after everything he'd already been suspected of.

He jumped out and ran to grab a wheelchair, then lifted Jemma into it. "Take her inside," he said to Raven. "I'm going to park the car."

He found a space at the far end of the parking lot and was about to climb out when he spotted a squad car pulling in. Sinking down in his seat, he waited until the two officers went inside. They would likely go straight to Jemma to interview her first. He needed to talk to Raven—make sure she had her story straight. The police might try to trip her up and pin this on him.

He walked through the automatic doors and glanced around the waiting room. There was no sign of Raven or Jemma, or the police officers. He hurried over to the reception desk. "Excuse me, my daughter, Raven Golding, just came in with a head injury. Can I see her, please?"

The receptionist threw a furtive glance at her associate before getting to her feet. "One minute, Mr. Golding. I'll check on her."

He leaned across the desk, painting on a woebegone expression. "Can you just tell me which room she's in?"

The woman pinched her lips together. "If you give me a minute, I'll be happy to assist you."

She marched out from behind the desk and disappeared down the hallway. When she reappeared, there was a police officer by her side.

"Mr. Golding, I'm Officer Hendricks. I'd like to ask you a few questions."

Andrew furrowed his brow. "I want to see my daughter, first."

The officer cleared his throat. "I'm afraid that won't be possible until after we take your statement. We need to interview all three of you separately. Detective Meehan is en route. Until then, the best I can do is give you an update on your daughter's condition. I can assure you, she's being well taken care of."

Andrew curled his fingers into fists. He had known the police wouldn't take their account at face value. It was too preposterous. He'd had an affair with a student who had gone missing, presumed dead, and now he had mysteriously found her, and rescued her from captivity by his wife's new employee—a girl who had gone to high school with his estranged daughter. They were beginning to sound suspiciously like a crime family. Not to mention the fact that he still didn't know where his wife was.

"Can you at least find out what's going on with my daughter?"

"They've taken her for a CAT scan," Hendricks responded. "As soon as we get any news on her condition, you'll be the first to know." He turned to the receptionist. "Is there an office we can use nearby?"

She gave a curt nod. "Follow me." She marched them down the hallway and into a stuffy, windowless room. She gave Andrew a scorching look as she pulled the door closed behind her. He wilted a little on the inside. She had recognized him and wanted to convey her contempt. It wouldn't be long before everyone else did, too.

Hendricks pulled out a notebook and thumbed through it to a blank page. "Let's start with your full name and address."

Andrew rattled off the information in robotic mode. Should he ask for a lawyer? He wasn't under arrest and he hadn't committed a crime. Quite the opposite—he had solved a case. Theoretically, he was a hero. So why did he have a sinking feeling this was all about to go sideways?

45

RAVEN

Raven closed her eyes as her body slid into the CT scanner. She was immensely relieved that she and Jemma had made it out of Nikki's dungeon alive, and beyond grateful for the care she was being given, but her thoughts were with her mother. Where could she have gone last night? As desperate as she had been to mend their relationship, she would never intentionally ignore Raven's multiple texts and calls. Something was wrong.

Raven couldn't help thinking back to Gloria's strange behavior at the thrift store. There was no reason for her to be there that late at night. Was it possible she was involved in the scheme to blackmail her mother? But how could she have found out about her mom's past? And Gloria wasn't computer savvy. If she was blackmailing her mother, she must have a partner in crime. Had she been working with Nikki all this time? Maybe Gloria had recommended her for the position to begin with. That would explain why her mother had been willing to hire someone who lived so far from the store.

Raven's head pounded as her thoughts spun. Even with

the pain medication the nurse had given her, the jackhammering of the CT scanner was pushing her to her breaking point. She desperately wanted to be with her dad. The euphoria she had felt on seeing him screech to a stop on the street at her moment of greatest need had melted away any lingering rancor. She was surprised at how emotional she felt about a man who had let her down so badly. But it wasn't as if she was anything but a flawed human being herself, with a past she wasn't particularly proud of either. Her reaction to the whole situation with her parents had been immature. She hadn't taken the time to sit down and listen to their side of the story or try to understand how they'd ended up in the situations they'd gotten into. Tears prickled her eyes. Would she ever get the chance now? Would she ever see her mother again?

Just when she thought she couldn't take the noise a minute longer, a voice came over the CT speaker. "Very good, Raven, we're all done. Great job."

Slowly, the narrow bed she was lying on moved back out from the cylindrical cube she'd been trapped in for the last half hour. A nurse assisted her into a wheelchair and took her to an examination room. She stiffened when she saw the police officer standing by the bed. *Meehan*!

He gave a curt nod in her direction. "I'd like to ask you a few questions about your ordeal."

A shiver ran down her spine. This was the detective she'd turned the urn over to and told about her dad's affair. Where was her dad? Had they arrested him again?

The nurse helped her into bed and plumped up the pillows behind her, before exiting the room.

"How's Jemma doing?" Raven asked, trying to keep her voice steady.

"She's in surgery. She's going to be fine."

"Where's my dad?"

"He's waiting in another room. I need to talk to you separately, first."

She took a few shallow breaths, trying to read between the lines. Would he try to get her to say something to incriminate her father? Surely the police must believe Jemma's account of things—assuming she'd told them the truth.

Meehan rubbed his chin, as though waiting on her to say something.

She arched a questioning brow. "Do I need a lawyer?"

He gave her a flat smile, betraying nothing. "That's entirely up to you. I just have a few questions to straighten out some facts."

She shrugged. "So long as you make it quick. My head's pounding."

"It won't take long, I promise. How did you know Jemma Knight was here in Bridgehaven?"

"I didn't. I went there to—" She broke off mid-sentence, suddenly aware that she couldn't reveal the real reason she'd gone to Nikki's place without getting her dad into more trouble than he was already in.

Meehan's laser-focused gaze remained pinned on her. "You were saying?"

She inhaled lightly through her nostrils, trying to calm her breathing. She wasn't about to tell him her mother was missing, or confess to her computer hacking stunt, but she had to give him something. "Nikki and I went to high school together. We didn't have a good relationship—to put it mildly. When I found out she'd started working for my mother, I wanted to know what her motive was. I went to her house to confront her."

Meehan raised his brows a fraction. "Why drive all the

way to her place at that time of night? You could have talked to her at the thrift store, or picked up the phone and called her."

Raven scrunched the cotton sheet in her fist, searching for a response that sounded halfway reasonable. Her brain was fogging over again.

Meehan leaned back in his chair and folded his arms in front of him, observing her for a moment. "Perhaps she was expecting you."

Raven frowned. "What's that supposed to mean?"

"Maybe it was your idea to kidnap Jemma to punish your father, and it all went horribly wrong when Nikki refused to let her go."

46

RAVEN

Raven had requested a lawyer, and Meehan left shortly after that. She was fairly certain he'd just been fishing with his insinuation that she was involved in Jemma's abduction, but she wasn't about to take the chance of being dragged into this investigation as anything other than a victim.

By the time she was discharged from the hospital, it was midmorning the following day. She and her dad drove home in blissful silence. The dizzying sights and sounds of the hospital had only compounded the pain in her head, and she wanted nothing more than to go home and drink a cup of tea in peace. The results of the CT scan were reassuring—no bleeding on the brain, only a goose egg on her head that would need to be handled with care for the next few days.

Thankfully, Jemma had come through her surgery with no complications and was going to be fine. They had stopped in to see her, but they hadn't stayed long once they found out her parents were at the hospital and had only stepped out to grab breakfast. Raven doubted they would be thrilled to see her or her father, despite the fact that they had rescued Jemma—possibly saved her life. It could never undo what Andrew Golding had done to their daughter. Rescuing her from Nikki wouldn't have been necessary in the first place, if he hadn't betrayed the university's code of conduct and taken advantage of a student under his tutelage.

A teary-eyed Jemma, on the other hand, had been grateful. She seemed genuinely remorseful for the disappearing stunt she had pulled, subjecting Andrew to a cloud of suspicion that had cost him his career. To his credit, he placed the blame firmly on himself for everything that had ensued.

Raven let out a sigh of relief at the welcome sight of her childhood home. She could hardly believe she had vowed never to set foot in it again. Right now, it felt like a refuge in the midst of a nightmarish chain of events.

"It feels good to be home," she said, as her dad pulled into the garage.

He twisted his lips. "I wish I could say the same. Technically, this isn't my home anymore."

Raven threw him a reproving look. "You can't think like that. Maybe Mom will relent now that Jemma's been found."

Her dad looked somber. "We need to concentrate on finding your mom now. I'm really worried about her. If we haven't heard from her by noon, we'll have to report her missing. I'm mentally preparing to be arrested a second time."

"I thought that detective was going to arrest me at the hospital—he as good as suggested it was my idea to kidnap Jemma."

"He was just making sure our stories jived, that's all."

Her dad climbed out, fussing over her like she was an invalid.

"What do you want for lunch?" he asked, once she was settled into the couch in the family room. "Does a grilled cheese sound good?"

"Sure. Can you bring me that note with the phone number from the office?"

He furrowed his brow. "First, you need to eat something. You didn't touch your breakfast at the hospital."

"I was too nauseous. But I'm feeling better now that I'm home."

He nodded. "Okay, chill for a few minutes, and I'll be back with your sandwich and that phone number."

She leaned her head back on the couch and closed her eyes. *I'm coming for you, Mom.* She had tried calling her on Dad's phone multiple times, but to no avail. She didn't want to alarm her dad, but she had a growing conviction that Mom was in trouble, and it had something to do with her drug-dealing ex-boyfriend. Raven was still feeling weak and her head ached, but if things were the other way around, her mother would come to her aid. If she'd been lying in the gutter shot up with drugs, Mom would have found her somehow and brought her home. Raven shared that resolve of steel. One way or another, she would get to the bottom of her mother's disappearance.

When her father returned with her grilled cheese sandwich, she began to salivate, surprised at how hungry she suddenly felt. She devoured the food, the calories lending her renewed energy and determination. "Thanks, Dad. I needed that." She wiped her mouth on a napkin and reached for the note he had set on the coffee table.

He laid a hand on hers. "Wait! Before you make that call, there's something important I need to tell you."

She jerked her head toward him, picking up on a thread of desperation in his voice. She'd forgotten he had something he wanted to talk to her about. "What is it?"

He sighed, brushing a shaking hand across his brow. "There's no easy way to say this. Raven, I just found out that your mom has ALS."

Her heart began to thud painfully in her chest. This felt like a bad dream after everything she'd lived through in the past few hours but, judging by the expression on her father's face, she hadn't misheard him. "When ... when did she tell you?"

"She didn't. Carmen told me. She was only diagnosed recently and she was planning to tell us before she went missing."

"How bad is it?"

He shook his head. "I don't know any details. She may not know too much herself, yet. She's going through tests and stuff."

"So it's not conclusive?"

Her dad bit his lip. "We have to stay positive. We need to concentrate on finding her first."

"And quickly." Raven snatched up the note from the table, the need to do something more acute than ever. If her time with her mom was limited, she didn't want to waste a minute of it.

"I already tried that number a couple of times while I was making your sandwich. No answer." Her dad rubbed a hand over his face and sighed. "It's been almost forty-eight hours. It's time we called the cops—let them arrest me if that's what they want to do."

Raven grimaced. "Let's give Carol one more try."

Her dad pursed his lips as he fished his phone from his pocket. "Read me off the number."

He hit the speaker button, then placed the phone on the coffee table between them. It rang and rang and, just as Raven had given up hope of speaking with the elusive Carol, a feeble voice said, "Hello?"

She shot forward to the edge of the couch. "This is Raven Golding. Is this … Carol?"

"I'm sorry. Can you speak up?" the woman answered. "I'm a little hard of hearing."

Raven picked up the phone and spoke directly into it, enunciating each word. "This is Raven, I'm Sage Golding's daughter. You might remember her as Sage Barker."

"Oh, hello, Sage dear. How are you?"

Raven shot her dad a frustrated look. "Carol, this is Sage's daughter, Raven," she bellowed into the phone.

"Oh, how nice of you to call. Have we met before?"

"No, we haven't. I'm calling to ask if you've talked with my mother recently?"

"As a matter of fact, Sage came by here last night. It was a real treat to see her after all these years. I must say, I was very surprised when—"

"Carol," Raven interrupted. "Is she still there with you?"

"What's that, dear?"

Raven raised her voice again. "Is my mom still at your place?"

"Oh no! She left last night. But she did stay for a while after I went to bed." Carol chuckled. "She hadn't seen my son in a long time. I'm sure they had a lot to talk about."

A steely finger of fear wrapped itself around Raven's chest, making it difficult to breathe. She had to ask the question hammering against her skull, even though she was sure she already knew the answer. She opened her mouth, but the words stuck in her throat.

Carol picked up where she'd left off, responding to the

unspoken question. "My boy and Sage used to date before he—. Well, anyway, suffice to say, I always had a soft spot for Sage. I hoped she and Jared might make me a grandma one day."

47

SAGE

Sage stumbled down the lane toward the gravel road, thankful that dawn was breaking, but nervous that it made her more visible. She considered jumping the fence and making her way through the fields, sticking close to the cover of the hedge, but it would take her twice as long, and there was a good chance she would end up twisting her ankle. Her only goal now was to reach the main road before Jared caught up with her, and flag down a passing car.

As she ran, she cast the occasional glance over her shoulder, fearful she would see a dark, malevolent shadow gaining on her, baring his teeth in an insidious grin, reveling in the knowledge that her end was coming—that she was at his mercy once more. Every tiny sound startled her, driving home the fear that she wasn't going to make it out of here alive—that she would never see her daughter or her husband again. There was nothing she wanted more than to hold them in her arms, warts and all. Facing death on multiple fronts had made it abundantly clear to her that everything in their broken relationships could be forgiven.

Relief pumped through her veins like a shot of adrenaline when she reached the bottom of the lane without any sign of Jared in pursuit. She ran the whole way down the gravel road and darted straight out onto the main road, glancing desperately in both directions. Which way? Just as she was about to take off running again, she spotted a truck rounding the bend. Her heart leapt up her throat. Holding her ground, she waved frantically to flag the vehicle down. The risk of being mowed down in the middle of the road was infinitely preferable to being left behind at the mercy of a monster. To her immense relief, the beat-up truck swerved suddenly and pulled over to the side of the road, brakes screaming. The driver, a buff, good-looking kid in his early twenties, rolled down his window. "Need a ride?"

"Yes, please," she blurted out, dashing over to the passenger side and climbing in.

"Did your car break down or something?" His deep clay-colored eyes traveled over her, taking in her unkempt appearance. "Are you all right?"

"Yes, I'm fine, thanks," she gasped. "Just ... just take me to the nearest police station, please. Can I borrow your phone?"

"I left it charging at the house," he replied, shifting the truck into gear. "I'm just running a quick errand."

He pulled back onto the road, but instead of heading into town, he turned onto the gravel road leading back to the abandoned farm.

"Where are you going?" Sage cried out in alarm. "This is the wrong way."

The man ignored her and kept driving, staring straight ahead. Sage braced herself as the truck bobbed up and down, the aging suspension doing little to absorb the ruts in the road. Terror raced through her when he turned onto the lane she had just run down. Why was he taking her back to the abandoned farmhouse? Was he one of Jared's junkie friends —here to buy drugs? Was that the quick errand he'd alluded to? Or had she climbed into the truck of a rapist seeking to take advantage of a stranded woman? Whatever the case, he didn't have good intentions, or he would have given her an explanation for their detour. She had to get out of here, fast.

She reached for the door handle, but a brutal fist to the side of her head left her stunned and nauseous.

"Try that again and I'll put a bullet in your head," the man growled.

She moaned, as the truck continued to shake its way up the lane. She stole a sideways glance at the man but couldn't spot a weapon bulging beneath his shirt. Was he bluffing? She couldn't count on it. Not if he was part of the circle Jared moved in. Drugs and guns went hand-in-hand, and he'd already displayed a propensity for violence. But she couldn't go back to that barn either. Not when she knew who was waiting for her.

She dived toward the door handle once more, but this time the man grabbed her by the hair and yanked her head back. She screamed in agony.

"I warned you!" he roared. He stepped on the gas, not letting go of her hair. She was sure it was going to come out by the roots as the truck thumped the rest of the way up the lane. They swerved to a halt behind the house, and he killed the engine and jumped out, dragging her with him. "Inside," he barked, shoving her in the direction of the rotting front door.

For the second time in the space of an hour, Sage stepped inside the dilapidated house. The man pushed her onto one of the dirty mattresses and stood over her, lighting up a cigarette. Her stomach roiled as she tried not to imagine what his intentions were.

"What do you want? Is it money?" she cried. She rummaged in her purse and pulled out all the cash she had, thrusting it at him. "Here, you can have it. Buy yourself some more drugs. Just let me go. I won't go to the police. I don't care about your drug squatting parties or whatever it is you do here."

He laughed, took another puff of his cigarette as he scooped up the cash and ran a greedy eye over it. "I reckon you could cough up a lot more than that." A sly grin crept over his lips. "You've been putting out pretty good up until now."

48

SAGE

Sage stared at the stranger in shocked silence. A creeping feeling of dread came over her. Was he talking about the blackmail? Was this the person who had siphoned off thirty thousand dollars of her money and counting? But how did he know she was the snitch? Only one explanation came to mind.

"You're ... working with Jared." It wasn't a question, more of an admission to herself that her fate was sealed.

He tapped the ash from his cigarette with practiced ease, an amused smile on his lips. "That's right, Einstein."

Sage swallowed hard. Her situation had gone from bad to terminal in a heartbeat. The minute he discovered what she'd done to Jared, there was no telling what he would unleash on her in return. She had to keep him talking—develop a rapport, anything to keep him away from the barn until she could figure out a plan.

She softened her expression. "What's your name?"

He adjusted his stance with a loose-legged swagger. "You can call me TJ."

She nodded. "My name's Sage, but maybe you already

know that. What you don't know is that I have a terminal disease. I may not have much time left." She sat up a little straighter on the mattress, wincing in pain. "My family needs me. I have a husband and a twenty-year-old daughter. They must be worried sick about me, by now. If you let me go, I promise I won't press charges. I won't even make a police report about anything that's happened. I just want to go home to my family."

TJ tossed his cigarette butt on the floor and stomped it out with his boot. "That's for Jared to decide when he gets back. What I want to know is how you escaped? He must have tied you up before he took off."

Sage hesitated. "He didn't restrain me. He ... he made me drink something. When I woke up, I was lying on one of these mattresses. His car was gone so I figured he'd decided to let me go."

TJ's eyes narrowed. "Jared would never let you go. He's been waiting a long time for this."

Without warning, he yanked her to her feet. "We're gonna take a little walk."

"Wait! Where are you taking me?" she asked, fighting to keep the panic out of her voice.

"I'm tying you up where you belong. In the barn. You're not gonna make a break for it a second time."

"No! Wait! Please don't. I'll get you whatever amount of money you want—just let me go. You can have it all. You don't even have to share it with Jared. He doesn't need to know."

TJ laughed. "No one double-crosses Jared and lives to tell about it."

She fought all the way as TJ frogmarched her out of the house and across the yard into the barn. Her heart almost stopped when he forced her through the doorway. To her surprise, Jared was still lying prone on the floor in the same position she'd left him in. The chair he'd tied her to lay next to him along with the rope. Her pulse raced in her throat. Had she killed him? Had the tranquilizer dose been too strong? She'd made her best estimate, but she'd been in a blind panic, not to mention the fact that she wasn't a veterinarian—she could have been way off.

"What did you do to him?" TJ snarled, shoving her across the floor.

Grabbing the discarded rope, he secured her wrists to the horse stall rail before dropping to his knees next to Jared and shaking him by the shoulders. "Hey, man! *Jared*! Can you hear me?" When there was no response, he jumped to his feet and darted a glance around the barn, before disappearing outside.

Sage's heart shot halfway up her throat. Was her life about to end in an abandoned building? She had escaped once, but she wouldn't be so lucky a second time. When Jared came around, he would finish her off, and if he didn't regain consciousness, TJ could be counted on to do the job on his behalf.

A moment later, he came running back inside with a bucket of water in hand. He threw it over Jared, then sank back down next to him and shook him again. To Sage's horror, he began to stir. She watched like a frozen rabbit feigning death as TJ helped him into a sitting position. He shook the water from his hair like a monster emerging from the murky, ocean depths.

TJ gripped him by the forearm and pulled him to his feet. "You okay, man?"

Jared gave a terse nod, running a hand over the back of his neck. "Do you have my gun?"

TJ frowned. "No, haven't seen it."

Jared yanked up the leg of his jeans and stared at his empty ankle hilt.

Slowly, he lifted his head, his gaze settling on Sage. His eyes bored into her, like burning coals branding her guilt.

She went limp, sagging against the stall. Her time had come.

49

SAGE

Sage's entire body began to shake as Jared walked unsteadily over to her. She yanked at the bonds on her wrists—a futile attempt to stave off the inevitable. Jared reached for her throat and squeezed. Her eyes bulged as she strained in vain to take a breath. She was sure he was about to finish what he'd started, but he suddenly shook her and thrust her away from him with a growl of disgust.

"Where's my gun?"

"I … I threw it into the ditch behind the house."

"And my knife?"

Sage dropped her head. "Same."

He rubbed the spot on his arm where she'd jabbed him, eying her with suspicion. "Didn't think you had the guts to try and kill me. What did you stick me with—poison?"

"It was only a sedative," Sage mumbled.

Jared grunted and yanked her chin up, forcing her to look him in the eye. "So now you're treating me like one of your wretched rescue dogs. You told me you loved me once."

"I did," she sobbed. "You were my world."

"So why'd you sell me out to the cops?"

"I didn't—"

Jared clapped a hand over her mouth, his grip almost suffocating her. "Don't lie to me!" he hissed in her face. "I know it was you! Why else would you pay up? You couldn't risk anyone finding out your dirty little secret. You sold me out to the cops—framed me for murder. I've suspected it for years. I could have made a phone call from prison to any one of a dozen people and had them knock you off a long time ago."

"So why didn't you?" Sage croaked.

"Maybe I kept hoping it wasn't true. I needed to hear you admit it before I could believe it." He grabbed her by the chin again and squeezed it hard, jerking it side to side. "This is the face I waited thirty years to see. But I knew the minute I looked into your eyes that you were lying to me." He shook his head. "You shouldn't have come by the house. Bad mistake."

"What ... what are you going to do?"

He glanced away. "Something I hoped I'd never have to do."

"Jared, please. You don't have to do this. You won't get away with it. It will break your mother's heart if you go back to prison."

He set his lips in a tight line. "That's not going to happen. I'll bury you someplace no one will ever find you."

"Please, Jared. You can have my money—all of it. I already told TJ that."

"TJ, huh?" Jared glanced over at him, standing off to one side, and laughed. "That's Tyler, my nephew. I thought you two knew each other."

Sage shot him a confused look. "I've never seen him before in my life."

Tyler walked over to them, arms folded in front of his chest. A disturbing sneer slid over his lips. "We never officially met. I dated your daughter."

A creeping realization prickled Sage's skin. Raven had mentioned a boyfriend—tatted up and unemployed—but she'd never introduced him. Sage hadn't liked the sound of him and, as far as she knew, the relationship hadn't lasted long. Maybe she could appeal to him.

"Why are you going along with this, Tyler? You must have had some feelings for Raven. Don't you care that your uncle is threatening to kill me?"

Jared and Tyler exchanged amused glances.

"The only feelings Tyler has are the ones I tell him to have," Jared said. "I hired him for a job—to find out if Raven knew what you'd done. I thought mothers and daughters had the kind of relationship where they talked about everything. But apparently you two weren't that close."

Sage's face crumpled. "I suppose you were behind the anonymous message my daughter received."

Tyler tilted his chin upward, a triumphant glint in his eyes. "It got her attention. She poked around on your husband's computer, and yours. When she found the blackmail threats, she finally realized what a fake you are."

Jared let out a scathing snort. "But she might still be willing to do something to save your life."

Blood drained from Sage's head. At all costs, she had to protect Raven. "Leave my daughter out of this."

Jared scratched the stubble on his jaw. "She won't be harmed if she does what she's told. Your job is to call her up and have her transfer the money out of your accounts."

"You don't need to get her involved in this. I can get you the money."

Jared's expression morphed into one of faux pity. "I think

you know by now you're not leaving this barn alive. If you don't do it my way, Tyler will be digging your daughter's grave too."

"No! Jared, please! This has nothing to do with Raven."

He nodded to Tyler. "Go look for my gun and knife."

Tyler gave a curt nod and turned on his heel.

"Alone at last." Jared sneered at her. "But not for long. I'm going to untie you so you can make that call. If you try anything, the rope goes around your neck this time. Do you understand?"

Sage nodded mutely. The thought of anything even touching her raw neck again made death the preferable option.

Jared loosened her bonds, then snapped the rope in front of her face, making her flinch. A chilling reminder that his strength had returned, and he wouldn't hesitate to follow through on his threat if she deviated from his orders. He pulled out his phone. "What's her number?"

Sage recited it, each digit scraping across her injured throat as she tried not to burst into tears.

To her relief, the call went straight to voicemail. Jared tried the number several more times, glaring at her. "Are you messing with me?"

"No! We're ... not on good terms. She doesn't always take my call."

Jared scowled. "Plan B. What's your husband's number?"

Sage's bottom lip trembled as she watched him punch it in, but she'd rather put Andrew's life at risk than Raven's. She hated herself for even having the thought. The only consolation was that Andrew would agree with her.

50

RAVEN

Clutching the phone to her ear, Raven locked eyes with her dad's stricken gaze, giving him an almost indiscernible nod. It was just as they'd feared.

She cleared her throat, half-shouting into the phone. "Carol, could I speak with Jared?"

"He's not here right now, dear. I can have him call you when he gets in, if you like."

Raven's heart jackhammered in her chest. "Do you know where he is?"

Carol tinkled a laugh. "That boy never tells me where he's going. I suppose he is a grown man, but it's very awkward when I'm trying to cook dinner and—"

"Carol, I'm sorry to interrupt, but could I possibly have his phone number?"

"Jared doesn't have a cell phone, dear. He can't afford one. He's looking for work right now, but it's ... well, it's difficult when you have a record."

Raven rolled her eyes. Of course he would tell her that. He didn't want her tracking his movements, or giving his number to anyone who came looking for him. But his parole officer would have his number. There was nothing else to do but hack into the parole registry website and extract the information she needed. It was the only way she was going to be able to track down Jared, and her mom.

"Carol, I've got to run. It was lovely talking to you."

She hung up before the elderly woman could reroute the conversation again. "He has her, Dad. He knows what she did, and he's going to kill her if we don't find her in time."

He got to his feet, smoothing a hand over his ruffled hair. "We need to call the police."

She threw him a frustrated look. "We don't have time for that. Do you want to spend the next few hours being interrogated by skeptical officers who might decide to detain you on suspicion of kidnapping and murder, or do you want to spend it trying to save Mom's life? If we can locate her, then we can enlist their help getting her out of Jared's clutches."

He groaned, tenting his hands over his nose. "How soon can you get that phone number?"

Raven jumped to her feet. "Let's find out."

In the office, she logged onto the computer. Time was of the essence. She had to work quickly to identify a vulnerability in order to infiltrate the website. Best case scenario she would stumble across some kind of security misconfiguration—unpatched software, an admin port left open, or some such careless mistake. Theoretically, it should be more difficult to hack into a government website built with a high level of technical expertise, but human error was rife, and governmental institutions struggled to detect and fix their own programming flaws. Raven could feel the adrenaline flooding her brain as she immersed herself in the task of penetrating the maze of the parole registry website.

"Can I do anything to help?" her father asked, cupping

his hands behind his head. Raven cast a glance his way. He looked helpless outside of his flowing academic robes that leant him an air of authority.

"You can make me a strong cup of black coffee," she said, with a bolstering grin.

A measure of relief flooded his face at the petty assignment. She felt sorry for him. His entire world had crumbled. Granted, he had brought it on himself, but they all had a stake in this mess. It would take them banding together as a family to crawl back out of it.

When he returned a few minutes later, he set a steaming mug down on the desk and gave her a hesitant smile. "Making progress?"

She nodded, her eyes fixated on the screen. "Yes, but this could take a while. Why don't you call Carmen and ask her if she can bring my car over. You can give her a ride back to her place." She reached for her coffee. "That would be helpful." It would also mean he wouldn't be hovering over her shoulder the entire time she was trying to concentrate.

"Of course. I'll leave you to work in peace."

She tapped steadily on the keyboard, registering muffled voices in the background when Carmen arrived, then blissful silence. When her dad returned, a short time later, he stuck his head around the door, gave a quick wave, and retreated without interrupting her. In total, it took her a little under two hours to break in and access the parole record retrievals.

It appeared Jared Brogan had been the beneficiary of a discretionary parole after completing a substance-abuse program and vocational training, and managing to convince the members of the parole board that he was fit to re-enter society as a reformed character. What a joke! His time in prison had only honed his lawbreaking skills.

She quickly drilled down on Jared's personal details and retrieved the phone number he had listed with his parole officer. Bingo! "Dad! I've got it!"

He came running back into the office, a hopeful look in his eyes. "Now what? Do we call him?"

Raven shook her head. "Let me see your phone. I need to download a location tracking app."

He fished it out of his pocket and passed it to her.

With the app downloaded, she entered Jared's phone number, chewing on her lip until a green circle appeared on the screen. "There he is! Northburg Township—about an hour from here." She jumped to her feet and snatched up her sweatshirt from the back of the chair.

"You sure you're up for the journey?" her dad asked. "Maybe I should go alone."

Raven snorted. "Not a chance. We're in this together."

"I don't want you trying any of your jiu-jitsu moves on him."

"Don't worry, I'm not going to engage with a convicted murderer. If he has Mom, we'll call the police. Do you have gas in your car?"

He nodded. "You can navigate."

He peeled out of the garage and tore off down the road at a speed Raven had never seen him drive at before.

"Take it easy, Dad. The last thing we need is to get pulled over."

They were halfway to Northburg Township when his phone began to ring. She glanced at it nestled in the console. "Unknown number. Want me to pick up?"

Her dad grimaced. "Not really. It could be the dean calling to ask me to pack up my office and be out by the end of the day."

"Or it might be Detective Meehan following up on Mom.

We should answer it. If it's the dean, I'll tell him you're not available."

Her dad gave a glum nod. "Go ahead."

Raven reached for the phone and slid her finger across the screen. "Hello?"

For a moment, there was only the sound of breathing, and then she heard a raspy voice.

51

RAVEN

"Mom?" Raven's voice trembled. "Mom, is that you?"

"Yes, it's me, honey, where are you?"

Raven shot her dad a questioning look. He shook his head.

She squeezed her eyes shut and tried to think. She couldn't give any indication of their intentions—no doubt Jared was listening to every word. "Um ... driving ... to the store."

"Where's your father?"

"He's here, in the car with me. Mom, where are you? Are you okay?"

"I'm fine. I need you to listen to me for a minute. I want you and Dad to go to Legacy First Bank and transfer all the money from our accounts—savings and checking."

Raven's stomach knotted. "Mom, is Jared making you do this?"

"Everything's going to be all right. He'll let me go, if you do exactly what I say. Please, Raven. I'm begging you."

She cast a sideways glance at her dad. A sheen of sweat

glistened on his forehead. He was driving at least fifteen miles over the speed limit, but she no longer cared. They had to reach Mom before it was too late.

"Okay, I'll do it."

Her mother let out a shuddering sigh of relief. "How long will it take you to get there?"

"Let me check the GPS for the nearest branch." She waited for a heartbeat, pretending to be consulting her phone. "Looks like there's one five minutes from here."

Raven could hear muffled voices in the background. There was a long pause before her mother spoke again, "Do you have a pen to write down the account information for the transfer?"

Her dad gestured toward the glove box. Raven grabbed a pen and an old receipt. "Okay, go ahead."

She scribbled down the routing and account numbers her mother recited to her. Maybe the police could trace them later.

"Call me back on this number as soon as the transfers have been made," her mother said. "I love—"

"Wait!" Raven cried. The call ended abruptly, as though someone had snatched the phone from her mom's hand.

Her chest heaved up and down with emotion. "We know for sure he has her now."

Her dad gritted his teeth, hands clenched around the steering wheel. "Call Meehan."

Raven fished in her jeans pocket for the business card the detective had given her and dialed the number.

"Detective Meehan speaking."

"Detective, it's Raven Golding."

"Raven, what can I do for you?" he asked in a businesslike tone.

"I know where my mom is. She's being held hostage."

There was a heartbeat of silence, before he responded, "By whom?"

"An ex-boyfriend of hers. He's been blackmailing her for the past month or so. He just got out of prison after serving thirty years for a drug-related murder." The words continued to tumble out in semi-coherent fashion, Meehan interjecting with the occasional question to clarify things. "Do you know if he's working alone?"

"I have no idea. He was right there with her the entire time she was talking. I couldn't ask her anything."

"Do you know if he's armed?"

"No idea. All I know is that he's going to kill her as soon as he gets his hands on the money," Raven answered. "She's pretending he'll let her go, but I can tell she's lying. I have the coordinates he's holding her at. It's in Northburg Township. I just sent you a pin. How quickly can you get there?"

"I'll deploy a SWAT team, thirty minutes out. And Raven, don't even think about driving out there. This could turn out to be a dangerous standoff situation. We'll do our very best to extract your mother unharmed."

Raven hung up and turned to her dad. "We're only two minutes out. We're not going to wait for them."

52

ANDREW

Andrew turned onto a rutted lane, following Raven's instructions. His blood chilled at the thought of what lay ahead of them. There was no guarantee a SWAT team, or even a professional negotiator, would be able to persuade Jared to let Sage go. And he wasn't about to wait around to find out. He was prepared to die to protect his wife and daughter, if it came down to it. He was banking on the assumption that Jared was working alone—this was a personal vendetta against Sage, after all. If he and Raven could surprise him, they might be able to overpower him.

"Let's ditch the car, Dad," Raven urged. "We'll go on foot the rest of the way. I don't want Jared to hear us coming."

He pulled over and parked next to a cattle gate. "Are you sure you don't want to wait here?"

Raven tossed him an annoyed look. "Don't ask me that again."

He raised his palms in an apologetic gesture. "All right, let's do this."

They climbed out and broke into a jog, slowing their

pace when an abandoned farmhouse came into view. Fear thrummed through Andrew's head. He had no doubt Raven could hold her own in a fight, but he couldn't risk her getting another concussion. He had to make sure he got between her and Jared if it came down to it.

"That must be his truck by the barn," he whispered. "Let's scout the perimeter, first, see if we can spot Mom through one of the windows. She might be tied up somewhere."

Raven nodded and led the way, motioning for him to follow.

Andrew's heart was pumping blood at a pace he'd never experienced before. He couldn't allow himself to envision the worst-case scenario—that Sage was already dead. He comforted himself with the thought that Jared wouldn't dispose of her before he had the money in hand. She was the only bargaining chip he had.

They crept in leaden silence toward the dilapidated house. The building looked uninhabitable. One corner of the moss-covered roof had caved in, and the yard was overgrown with weeds. It was a stretch to think Jared was living here. Silently, Andrew followed his daughter all the way around the perimeter, peering in through the dirty, broken windows as they went by. There was no sign of Sage anywhere, but someone had been using the space recently. Several soiled mattresses and the remnants of a drug shooting party were scattered about the place—empty cans and bottles, needles, and pipes.

He searched outside for something he could use as a weapon, his eye landing on a sturdy looking piece of wood. He picked it up and slapped it in the palm of his left hand.

Raven arched a questioning brow. "What are you planning on doing with that?"

He shrugged. "Just in case." He couldn't envision actually using it as a weapon, but it felt better to be prepared.

"Mom must be in there somewhere," Raven whispered. " Maybe she's locked in a closet, or a cellar, or something. I'll take a look around inside. Wait here and keep a look out to make sure no one's coming."

Andrew cast a quick glance over his shoulder, then nodded to Raven to go ahead. He crouched down behind a stack of old wooden pallets, watching her tread gingerly over the broken glass and trash by the doorway, moving as stealthily as a cat. When she disappeared inside, he turned his attention to the task of guarding the entryway, intermittently sweeping a gaze over the yard. Seconds ticked by, stretching into minutes. He couldn't hear the tread of Raven's footsteps walking around inside the house, but he didn't hear the unsettling sounds of screams or a scuffle either. Maybe that wasn't a good thing. What if Jared had snuck up behind her and put a hand over her mouth?

Just as he was about to go inside to check on her, a young man walked around the side of the barn in the direction of the house. Andrew froze, his eyes bulging. This couldn't be Jared Brogan. He only looked to be about Raven's age. Andrew's pulse quickened as the man drew closer. He sucked in a hard breath. Jared wasn't working alone, after all. The odds were stacked against him and Raven now. How many more people were on the premises? This might be some kind of hangout for felons. Were they cooking up drugs in the barn?

His heart drummed against his ribs as he searched for any indication of a weapon on the man's hip. He looked buffed out, fit, and strong. Andrew's best bet was to attack from behind. The element of surprise was his only hope of overpowering him. He weighed the wood in his hands, gauging the damage it would do. He would do anything to protect his daughter.

He remained motionless, listening to the sound of the man's boots crunching on broken glass as he crossed the threshold.

"Hello, Raven," he said, in a slow, contemptuous drawl. "Miss me?"

53

RAVEN

Raven spun around and stared at Tyler in disbelief. "You! What ... what are you doing here?"

"Business." He stepped closer, his lips curling into a sneer. "But I could be persuaded to mix it with pleasure. I'm impressed you managed to track us down."

"How did—" Her voice trailed off when she noticed a shadow closing in behind him. Picking up on her inadvertent cue, he instinctively clenched a fist, a heartbeat too late to stave off the attack. Seconds later, he let out a muffled grunt, crumpling to his knees as her dad brought the wood down hard on the back of his head. Raven stood frozen to the spot, scarcely able to comprehend that she'd just witnessed her erudite father putting Tyler out of commission with a two by four. Her head spun as she tried to make sense of this latest development. She hadn't expected Jared to have company, and certainly not her ex. How on earth had he gotten mixed up with Jared? Drugs, most likely.

She grimaced when she recalled the day Tyler had approached her outside of Starbucks. He'd been cocky, full of himself, extremely good looking in a bad boy kind of way, exactly the kind of boyfriend her parents would have hated for her to bring home—which is the only reason she'd agreed to go on a date with him to begin with. Looking at him slumped on the ground in front of her now, the dots were beginning to connect. It had been no coincidence; she had been targeted. He hadn't been interested in her—she had merely been a means to an end, a way for Jared to find out about her mom. Thinking back, Tyler had asked a lot of questions about Sage, but he'd shown little interest in her father—something she should have picked up on. How could she have been so stupid? Tyler must be one of Jared's informants, a newly inducted member of his criminal circle.

Shaking herself loose of the depressing truth, Raven sprang into action. She grabbed some bailing twine lying in the corner of the room and tossed it to her dad. "Tie him up. We can't risk him getting loose once he comes around. I'll look for a rag or something to stuff his mouth with." She hesitated and squeezed her dad's shoulder. "I'm proud of you."

His eyes glistened, and he quickly knelt and busied himself unwinding the twine.

Raven picked her way between the mattresses and debris and headed to one of the back bedrooms where she'd spotted some fraying curtains earlier. She yanked one of them off the rod, spluttering from the dust that rained down on her. *Gross!* She ripped the curtain into strips, then hurried back to where her dad was securing a still-unconscious Tyler's hands behind his back. Crumpling up a strip of curtain, she stuffed it into his mouth, then tied another strip around his face.

"What if he chokes?" her dad asked, eying her makeshift gag job dubiously.

She flapped a dismissive hand. “I doubt it'll even dampen his hollering if he comes around. We need to hurry. Mom's not anywhere in the house. Let's check the barn.”

They dragged Tyler away from the doorway and dumped him unceremoniously on a mattress before heading back outside.

"Any more wood scraps lying around?” Raven asked.

Her dad nodded. "Take this for now. I'll go grab another piece from the back of the house.”

She peered anxiously around the yard, her body tense and ready for action. Other than a blue jay squawking, there were no signs of life anywhere. She only hoped her mother was still alive. This was the kind of location where you could bury a body and hide what you'd done from the rest of the world. Her dad reappeared, clutching an even more ominous-looking piece of wood with several rusted nails jutting out of it. He bit his lip as he handed it to her. "Here, take this. I hope you don't have to use it, but just in case.”

She nodded her thanks, secretly wondering how much good it would do them. A stick of wood—nails or no nails—was not going to save them if Jared had a gun.

“Let's circle the barn first, try and get a peek inside to see what we're up against,” her dad suggested. “If this is a drug operation, Jared might have more people working for him.”

“I don't think it is. Otherwise he would have a lookout posted.” Raven frowned. “Unless that was Tyler.”

They moved stealthily toward the barn, then crept around the back.

“Look! Mom's car!” Raven whispered urgently. “She must have driven out here to meet Jared.”

“Or he could have forced her to drive here,” her dad answered.

Peering between some loose slats, Raven could just

about make out an assortment of rusted up farm machinery, including an antique tractor. "There's no sign of any movement, but let's work our way around to the other side. I think I see some stalls down at the far end."

They continued skulking around the perimeter, all the while casting furtive glances around them to make sure they weren't being watched or followed.

When they came to another gap in the wall, Raven pressed herself against the siding and peeked through it. She sucked in a sharp breath, her knees almost buckling beneath her. "I see Mom," she whispered. "She's tied up to the railing on one of the stalls."

Her dad tented his hands over his eyes and squinted through the gap. "I don't see Jared anywhere. This could be our chance. But we need to be careful. He might be elsewhere on the property."

Raven prodded her dad forward. "Hurry! Let's get in and back out before he shows up."

They tiptoed around to the dilapidated barn door. Raven nudged it open slowly, praying it wouldn't squeak.

"I'll go first this time," her dad said, pushing past her before she could argue with him. She gripped her makeshift weapon and followed him inside. They froze at the sight of Jared dragging Sage over to a chair in the middle of the barn floor. Hearing their footsteps, he swung around to face them. Raven tensed, ready to spring into action, but her dad was already charging across the barn to tackle him. Eyes glinting, Jared released Sage with a violent shove to the floor.

Raven watched as her dad raised the two by four, preparing to swing, but she could already tell he'd mistimed it. With a roar of rage, Jared wrenched the wood from his hand and slugged him mercilessly with it. She caught her breath as he fell motionless to the ground.

With a grunt of satisfaction, Jared turned his attention to her, slapping the two by four menacingly against the palm of his hand.

Out of the corner of her eye, she caught a flurry of movement. Her mother was reaching for something beneath a tarp. Raven remained glued to the spot, her gaze firmly locked with Jared's. This time she wouldn't make the mistake of alerting her adversary.

54

SAGE

Sage pointed the gun she'd retrieved from beneath the tarp squarely at Jared. "What was that you were saying about burying my body where no one would find it?" Her voice held steady, despite the fact that her husband was lying at her feet, unconscious, possibly dead, and her heart was racing ninety miles an hour. An otherworldly calm counteracted her fear. Her family had come for her. It was all the fuel she needed. Somehow, Raven must have managed to track Jared's phone. It was the only possible explanation. She had always known her daughter was gifted, but she'd never understood quite how life-changing her talents could be, until now.

"You don't want to do this, Sage." Jared raised his meaty hands in the air, at odds with the defiant glint in his eyes.

She ignored his plea, keeping the gun trained on his chest. "Raven, call 911."

"The police are already on their way," she replied. "I'll get an ambulance coming." She darted over to her dad and fished his phone out of his pocket.

"Be reasonable, Sage." Jared took a hesitant step toward her. "Put down the gun. You don't know what you're doing."

"Move again and I'll shoot you."

"You wouldn't dare!"

"You don't intimidate me. I'd be happy to put you back in handcuffs."

He gave her a crooked grin. "Baby, I already told you I'm not going back to jail."

"Shut up and get down on the floor! On your belly, now!" she snapped, trying to ignore the searing pain in her throat.

Motionless, he held her gaze, like a snake trying to mesmerize her.

In the background, she could hear Raven talking to the emergency dispatcher. She didn't know if Jared would do what she'd told him to, and she wasn't sure she could bring herself to shoot him if he charged her. At all costs, she had to protect her daughter. She couldn't allow Jared to get the upper hand again—he wouldn't hesitate to kill her child and make her watch.

For a few tense moments, they stared at each other. She tried to visualize what her next move would be if he bolted. Should she shoot him in the leg? It might only enrage him. Maybe she should aim for the torso. If she killed him, she could claim self-defense. She had a witness in Raven.

As if reading her thoughts, Jared suddenly sank to his knees, then slowly stretched out on his belly. She kept the gun pointed at him, surprised that her hands weren't shaking as badly as she'd thought.

"Five minutes out," Raven said, running over to her. She dropped to the ground and placed her head on her dad's chest. "He's breathing." She gestured to Jared. "Do you want me to tie him up? There's bailing twine in the house."

Sage pressed her lips together. She couldn't risk giving Jared the opportunity to get his arm around Raven's neck—he would crush her windpipe in a heartbeat. "No. I'll keep the gun on him 'till the cops get here. You look after your dad."

Raven cradled his head in her hands. "Dad, can you hear me?"

Sage chanced a quick glance down at her daughter, shocked by the dried patch of blood on her head. "What happened to you?"

"Nikki clocked me with a dumbbell. I'm fine, I got checked out at the hospital already. I'm more concerned about dad—he's bleeding. I could grab the first aid kit from his car and dress the wound. We parked down the lane a bit—it's not too far."

Sage shook her head. "No. Tyler's still out there somewhere."

"Dad put him out of commission. He whacked him with a piece of wood and knocked him out cold. We tied him up. He won't be a problem, even if he comes around."

Sage blinked in disbelief. Perhaps she'd underestimated her husband's aspirations of valor. "Okay, but be careful."

Raven threw an uneasy glance at Jared lying prostrate on the floor, a reptilian blink the only indication that he was tuning in to their conversation. "Sure you got this under control, Mom?"

"Yes! Go! But be quick!"

Raven sprinted over to the barn door, casting one last glance over her shoulder before disappearing outside.

"Don't put me through this again," Jared said in a wheedling voice. "You know I can't go back inside. You already robbed me of the best years of my life."

Sage adjusted her cramped finger on the trigger. "No, Jared! You did that to yourself."

"We both know I didn't kill Viper. You sold me out—made me pay for his murder. Why? Was it to protect someone?"

Sage shifted her stance, her chest tightening as buried emotions began to resurface. "Who do you think I was protecting? You left me to die at his hands when the sale went sideways. I was only another drug mule to you, nothing more. I had no choice."

Jared narrowed his eyes. "*You*? You shot Viper."

Sage heaved in a few panicked gasps, her lungs burning as painful memories flooded back to mind. "He came looking for you that night. He wanted his money. It was me or him—self-defense. But no one would have believed a junkie like me. I figured you deserved to pay for all the other murders you got away—"

She broke off at the sound of Andrew emitting the faintest of moans. For a flicker of a heartbeat, she glanced down at him. It was long enough. Like a caged cat, Jared sprang to his feet in one seamless move and bolted for the door.

Sage followed his retreating figure with the barrel of the gun. Carol's lined face floated to mind. Jared was her only child. It would destroy her if he died. But Sage couldn't let him go. She couldn't live with the fear of him showing up in the middle of the night to take revenge, or worse—go after her child. Clenching her teeth, she fired once, hitting him in the leg.

He howled but limped out the door anyway. For a long moment, Sage froze, before kicking into gear and hurrying after him. By the time she exited the barn, he was already in Tyler's truck, the engine roaring to life.

"Raven! Where are you?" Sage screamed, her eyes frantically scanning the area around the barn.

The truck wheels spun as Jared tore out of the yard.

Sage's heart surged up her throat as the sickening realization hit her. She aimed at the cab, then lowered the gun and watched as the truck disappeared in a cloud of dust.

She couldn't risk killing her daughter.

55

RAVEN

When Raven came to, she was folded over on the floor in the passenger side of Tyler's truck. A flash of confusion, and then it all came back to her. Jared had taken her by surprise—slammed straight into her. He'd grabbed her with almost superhuman strength, dragged her over to the truck and smashed her head against the door. She had no recollection of him throwing her inside.

She peered cautiously up at him, not wanting to alert him to the fact that she was conscious. He was hunched over the steering wheel, his face a menacing scroll of concentration as he throttled down the lane. She tried, surreptitiously, to brace herself against the bumps. Her head throbbed, she could already feel another knot forming, but there was no time to feel sorry for herself. She needed to collect her thoughts and figure out how to get out of this predicament.

Her right leg had fallen asleep, and her entire body was cramping. She wasn't sure she would be able to stand, let alone run, if she got an opportunity to make a break for it. Where was Jared taking her—did he even have a plan? If he thought he could use her as a hostage to lure Sage into taking her place, he had another thing coming.

She eyed the door handle, calculating her odds. Could she get it open and throw herself out on the road before Jared grabbed hold of her? More important, would she be able to get away from him even if she managed to exit the truck? Ordinarily, she would have rated the odds as good. But she was injured, and stiff. And there was a possibility she might sustain more injuries if she threw herself out of a moving vehicle. It was a chance worth taking. If Jared made it out to the main road before the police intercepted him, she was doomed. Tossing herself out of the truck at eighty miles an hour would be a lot deadlier than chancing it here on the dirt lane.

Resigned to the only course of action open to her, she visualized the possible scenarios that could unfold. If she injured herself jumping out, she could crawl beneath the hedge and hide, in the hope he would keep going. If she was able to run, she would head straight back up the lane to the barn. Jared was unlikely to turn around and pursue her, knowing her mom had his gun. Her eyes traveled slowly about the interior of the truck. Did Tyler have a weapon stashed in here—a switchblade or something? Possibly, even a gun. Jared might have already taken possession of it. He could shoot her if she reached for the door. But she was running out of time, as well as options. She had to make a move, or she would be trapped, and at his mercy. She took a few silent breaths, mentally pumping up her courage. As she was about to reach for the handle, she heard the unmistakable sound of sirens in the distance. *Finally!* But the police could still be a mile out. She had to stop Jared from getting away before the SWAT team turned onto the gravel road. Change of plan.

Before she could second-guess herself, she lunged for the steering wheel and jammed it hard to the left. Jared let out a frenzied roar, but she'd caught him off guard—he reacted too late to correct the wheel. The truck went straight through the ditch and into the barbed wire fence bordering the fields. Raven scrambled for the door, kicking Jared in the face as she leapt out onto the lane.

Without as much as a backward glance, she ran for her life, certain that any minute a bullet would strike her down, or a heavy hand would grab her from behind and tackle her to the ground. The sirens were louder now. Out of her peripheral vision she glimpsed flashing lights.

Jared had nowhere left to run.

56

SAGE

Sage screamed her daughter's name repeatedly, hoping against hope that Jared hadn't taken her with him—that, somehow, she'd managed to duck and hide when she'd spotted him emerging from the barn.

"Raven, are you here?" Her voice cracked, partly from emotion, partly from the pain of almost being strangled to death. "He's gone. It's safe now." She peered behind a pile of corrugated steel, desperately hoping to spot her daughter crouching down out of sight, shaking like a leaf but safe—here with her mother where she belonged. As the minutes ticked by, the horrifying truth became apparent. Jared had kidnapped her daughter.

A sick wave of terror rode through her veins with pulse-pounding force. This was her fault. She should never have let Raven out of her sight. She had assured her she had everything under control, but she'd gotten distracted when Andrew had started to come around—let down her guard for a split second. She'd handed Jared the opportunity he'd been chomping at the bit for as he'd lain on his belly like a crocodile in a swamp, snout just below the surface of the water, waiting on the perfect moment to strike.

Myriad thoughts pummeled her mind. She was stranded. Was her daughter alive? Why were the cops taking so long? With a weary tread, she returned to the barn to check on Andrew. To her relief, he was sitting up on one elbow, rubbing his head.

He blinked at her in a dazed fashion. "Is Raven with you?" He peered past her to the door.

Sage wet her lips. "Jared took her in Tyler's truck."

Andrew's face blanched of color as he struggled to his feet. "We have to go after them. My car's parked down the lane."

Sage grimaced. "Raven took your keys. And I think Jared took mine."

He threw her an anguished look. "Maybe your keys are in the house. Tyler might know where they are."

She followed him out of the barn, on shaky legs. She wasn't optimistic, but anything was better than waiting on the police to show up.

Tyler was writhing around on a mattress when they entered the house. His eyes flashed with anger when he saw them, and he mumbled something unintelligible. Sage walked over to him and yanked down his gag. He immediately spat out the curtain scraps. "I almost choked to death," he hissed. "You're gonna pay for this."

"The police are on their way. You can take it up with them," Sage shot back. "Where are my car keys? If you cooperate, I'll put in a good word for you."

Tyler narrowed his eyes. "Where's my uncle?"

"Good question," Andrew folded his arms in front of him. "He took off in your truck and left you to face the music. Guess you won't be seeing him, or your truck, again."

Tyler scowled. "I don't believe you. He wouldn't leave without me."

Sage gave a hollow laugh. "You don't know him half as well as I do. He was only using you as long as you served his purpose. Jared doesn't care about anybody other than Jared. You're on your own."

Tyler's eyes flicked to the doorway and back. "Where's Raven?"

Sage bit her lip. She didn't want to give him any information he could use against them, but he needed to know what kind of a person his uncle really was. "He took her hostage. He's too much of a coward to go on the run without a human shield."

Tyler drew his brows together suspiciously. "Why should I believe you?"

"What do I have to gain by lying about my daughter being abducted by that monster?" Sage replied. "I wish more than anything it wasn't true."

At the sound of approaching sirens, they turned their heads in unison.

Sage gripped Andrew by the arm. "They're close. They're coming up the lane."

He grimaced. "Hopefully, not too late to save Raven."

Abandoning Tyler, they darted outside and ran to meet the squad cars pulling in. Meehan stepped out of the first car wearing a bulletproof vest, one hand on his holster. Sage tried to read the expression on his face, but it was a mask of professionalism, revealing nothing. He gave a tight nod in their direction, then opened the back door of the squad car.

Sage fell to her knees, screaming, when Raven tumbled out and ran into her open arms.

~

A QUICK FAVOR

Dear Reader,

I hope you enjoyed reading ***What You Wish For*** as much as I enjoyed writing it. Thank you for taking the time to check out my books and I would appreciate it from the bottom of my heart if you would leave a review on Amazon or Goodreads as it makes a HUGE difference in helping new readers find the series. Thank you!

To be the first to hear about my upcoming book releases, sales, and fun giveaways, join my newsletter at

https://normahinkens.-com/newsletter

and follow me on Twitter, Instagram and Facebook. Feel free to email me at norma@normahinkens.com with any feedback or comments. I LOVE hearing from readers. YOU are the reason I keep writing!

All my best,

Norma

THE BRIDAL SHOWER

Check out *The Bridal Shower*, *the third book in the* ***Wicked Ways Collection***!

Hiding toxic secrets comes at a price.

Eva Peretti plans on throwing her best friend, Cat, an unforgettable bridal shower at a remote country estate. But the night before the shower, Cat receives an ominous message: *Secrets will be revealed tomorrow. Will they be yours?*

Distraught, she calls Eva to find out if this is a game she has arranged, only to discover that all the bridesmaids received the same message and are equally shaken.

Fearful that someone is out to sabotage her wedding, but not knowing who, or why, Cat agrees to proceed with the shower. All goes well until she opens an anonymous gift and discovers a bloody knife buried beneath layers of white tissue paper. During the confusion that follows, things take an even more chilling turn when her future mother-in-law vanishes.

Is someone intent on derailing Cat's wedding, or are they protecting her from a toxic secret she knows nothing about?

- Settle in for a twisty tale with an electrifying ending! -

Will you enjoy The Bridal Shower? If you read any of my favorite psychological and domestic suspense thriller authors including K.L. Slater, Shalini Boland, Kiersten Modglin, Freida McFadden, Kathryn Croft, Lisa Gardner, Louise Jensen, Gregg Olsen, Mark Edwards, or Rachel Caine, the answer is a resounding yes!

WHAT TO READ NEXT

Ready for another thrilling read with shocking twists and a mind-blowing murder plot?

Explore my entire lineup of thrillers on Amazon or at **https://normahinkens.com/thrillers**

Do you enjoy reading across genres? I also write young adult science fiction and fantasy thrillers. You can find out more about those titles at **https://normahinkens.com/YAbooks**

BIOGRAPHY

NYT and USA Today bestselling author N. L. Hinkens writes twisty psychological suspense thrillers with unexpected endings. She's a travel junkie, coffee hound, and idea wrangler, in no particular order. She grew up in Ireland—land of legends and storytelling—and now resides in the US. Her work has won the Grand Prize Next Generation Indie Book Award for fiction, as well as numerous other awards. Check out her newsletter for hot new releases, stellar giveaways, exclusive content, behind the scenes and more.

https://normahinkens.com/newsletter

Follow her on Facebook for funnies, giveaways, cool stuff & more!

https://normahinkens.com/Facebook

BOOKS BY N. L. HINKENS

SHOP THE ENTIRE CATALOG HERE

https://normahinkens.com/thrillers

<u>VILLAINOUS VACATIONS COLLECTION</u>

- The Cabin Below
- You Will Never Leave
- Her Last Steps

<u>DOMESTIC DECEPTIONS COLLECTION</u>

- Never Tell Them
- I Know What You Did
- The Other Woman

<u>PAYBACK PASTS COLLECTION</u>

- The Class Reunion
- The Lies She Told
- Right Behind You

<u>TREACHEROUS TRIPS COLLECTION</u>

- Wrong Exit
- The Invitation
- While She Slept

<u>WICKED WAYS COLLECTION</u>

- All But Safe

- What You Wish For
- The Bridal Shower

NOVELLAS

- The Silent Surrogate

BOOKS BY NORMA HINKENS

I also write young adult science fiction and fantasy thrillers under Norma Hinkens.

https://normahinkens.com/YAbooks

The Undergrounders Series
Post-apocalyptic

- Immurement
- Embattlement
- Judgement

The Expulsion Project
Science Fiction

- Girl of Fire
- Girl of Stone
- Girl of Blood

Books by Norma Hinkens

The Keepers Chronicles
Epic Fantasy

- Opal of Light
- Onyx of Darkness
- Opus of Doom

FOLLOW NORMA

Follow Norma:

Sign up for her newsletter:

https://normahinkens.com/newsletter

Website:

https://normahinkens.com/

Facebook:

https://normahinkens.com/Facebook

Twitter

https://normahinkens.com/Twitter

Instagram

https://normahinkens.com/Instagram

Pinterest:

https://normahinkens.com/Pinterest

Made in the USA
Middletown, DE
24 May 2024

54797948R00156